THE APARTMENT

A Century of Russian History

Text by

ALEXANDRA LITVINA

Illustrations by

ANNA DESNITSKAYA

Translation by

ANTONINA W. BOUIS

Abrams Books for Young Readers • New York

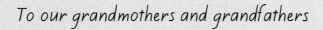

To our grandmothers and grandfathers

The illustrations in this book were made with watercolor, ink, Micron pens, and Photoshop.

Library of Congress Cataloging-in-Publication Data

Names: Litvina, Alexandra, author. | Desnitskaya, Anna, illustrator. | Bouis, Antonina W., translator.

Title: The apartment : a century of Russian history / text by Alexandra Litvina ; illustrations by Anna Desnitskaya ; translation by Antonina Bouis.

Other titles: Istoriia staroi kvartiry. English.

Description: New York : Abrams Books for Young Readers, 2019. | Originally published in Russia by Samokat Publishing House in 2017. |

Summary: Illustrations and text follow the story of a six-room Moscow apartment throughout the twentieth century and the family living there, as their personal upheavals and accomplishments reflect events in Russia and the wider world.

Identifiers: LCCN 2018037411 | ISBN 9781419734038

Subjects: | CYAC: Apartment houses—Fiction. | Family life—Fiction. | Russia (Federation)—History—20th century—Fiction.

Classification: LCC PZ7.1.L583 Ap 2019 | DDC [Fic]—dc23

Text copyright © 2016 Alexandra Litvina
Illustrations copyright © 2016 Anna Desnitskaya
Translated by Antonina W. Bouis
English translation © 2019 Abrams Books for Young Readers
Book design by Melissa J. Barrett

"Stanzas" by Joseph Brodsky. Copyright © 1962 and 1973 by Joseph Brodsky, as originally published in samizdat and currently collected in COLLECTED POEMS IN ENGLISH, used by permission of The Wylie Agency LLC.

Printed and bound in China
10 9 8 7 6 5 4 3 2 1

Abrams Books for Young Readers are available at special discounts when purchased in quantity for premiums and promotions as well as fundraising or educational use. Special editions can also be created to specification. For details, contact specialsales@abramsbooks.com or the address below.

Abrams® is a registered trademark of Harry N. Abrams, Inc.

ABRAMS The Art of Books
195 Broadway, New York, NY 10007
abramsbooks.com

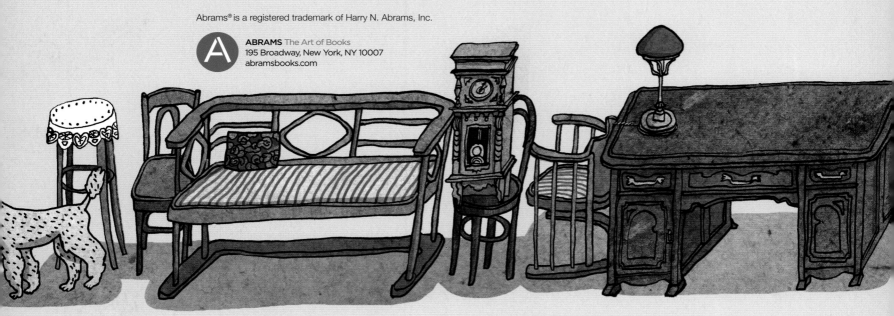

Not long before the Muromtsevs' moved to their new apartment, their furniture was delivered. It would live a long life there. Some things would last to the end of the twentieth century; others would not. Follow the life of the objects: which ones served their owners for a hundred years, and which ones vanished? What could have happened to them?

When you see a sign like this next to an object, look for it in the rooms on later pages.

ALLOW ME TO INTRODUCE THE MUROMTSEV FAMILY. WHERE EACH FAMILY MEMBER APPEARS IN THIS BOOK IS INDICATED BY THE PAGE NUMBERS IN PARENTHESES.

Ilya Stepanovich Muromtsev
1872—1942
(6, 8, 10, 16, 19, 22, 25, 29, 47)

Elena Nikolayevna Muromtseva
1874—1952
(6, 9, 10, 13, 15, 17, 19, 20, 25, 27, 47)

Maria Nikolayevna Volokhonskaya
1865—1918
(7, 8, 10)

François Dupuy
1890—1976

Irina Muromtseva
1896—1993
(6, 8, 10, 11, 15, 45, 47)

Sergei Voloshin
1892—1923
(8, 10, 15)

Nikolai (Nikolka, Nikolenka) Muromtsev
1907—1942
(8, 10, 11, 13, 15, 19, 21, 22, 29, 47)

Nelli Muromtseva
1910—1982
(21, 22, 25, 27, 30, 39)

Mark Dupuy
1930—2008

Sergo Ninoshvili
1921—2005
(27, 30, 35, 36, 39, 42, 45, 47, 50, 52)

Tamara (Toma) Muromtseva
1929—2005
(21, 23, 25, 27, 28, 30, 32, 34, 39, 42, 45, 47, 48, 51, 52)

Mikhail Kotlyar
1922—1943
(29)

Lida Muromtseva
1926—1975
(21, 23, 25, 27, 28, 30, 39)

Raisa Tikhomirova
1930—2010
(49)

Jean-Paul Dupuy
b. 1972
(52)

David Ninoshvili
b. 1963
(39, 40, 42, 45, 47, 52)

Genka Muromtsev
b. 1953
(34, 37, 39, 41, 42, 45, 49, 51, 52)

Tanya Muromtseva
b. 1953 (39, 41, 42, 45, 49, 51, 52)

Olya Ninoshvili
b. 1993
(52)

Trezor
(1898—1910)
(1, 2, 6)

Vaska
1900—1904
(7)

Strelka
1960—1978
(34, 39, 42)

4

Abram Naumovich
Shtein

1880–1941

(29)

Ester Girshevna Shtein

1886–1941

(29)

Efrosinia (Nanny)
Nikiforovna Shestova

1861–1932

(6, 10, 13, 15, 17, 19, 47)

Marfa Petrovna
Simonova (Cook)

1875–1920

(7, 9)

Marusya (Babmusya)
Muromtseva

1910–2009

(9, 10, 11, 13, 15, 16, 19, 20, 27,
28, 30, 33, 34, 39, 45, 52)

Nyuma (Veniamin,
Numa) Shtein

1906–1985

(20, 22, 30, 32, 34, 39)

Stepan Simonov

1895–1945

(19, 29)

Praskovya Simonova

1897–1976

(16, 19, 26)

Lena Shtein

1946–2011

(30, 33, 34, 37, 39, 52)

Friedrich (Fedya)
Shtein

b. 1937

(20, 27, 31, 33, 34, 36,
39, 40, 41, 42, 47, 52)

Katya Shtein

b. 1945

(47)

Antonina (Tonya) Simonova

1918–1980

(17, 18, 19, 26)

Petya Simonov

1917–1941

(17, 18, 19, 29)

Anya
Muromtseva

b. 1986

(45, 49, 51, 52)

Sasha
Muromtseva

b. 1979

(44, 47, 48, 51, 52)

Mitya (Mitka)
Muromtsev

b. 1975

(45, 46, 50, 52)

Sonya Muromtseva

b. 1974

(50, 52)

Jane (Zhenya) Shtein

b. 1978

(52)

Ilyusha Muromtsev

b. 1996

(52)

Murych

1990–2002

(49, 51)

Murzik

1950–1954

(30)

Mashka

1930–1939

(21, 22)

Trishka

1911–1915

(8, 10, 15)

5

Irina Muromtseva
October 12
1902

"Trezor! Tre-zor! Here, boy! Bad dog!"

Our poodle leaps out of the carriage and jumps around the unfamiliar porter, barking loudly. Papa would have been happy to grab Trezor by the collar, but Nanny's trunk is on his lap, and he can't move. We're moving into a new apartment in a big new building, which is why the porter is unfamiliar. He is as strong and respectable as Nikanor was in our old house on Samotechnaya Street and has the same full beard as Nikanor, too. This new porter is not at all frightened by Trezor. He ignores the dog and easily picks up Nanny's trunk and carries it up the stairs.

The new apartment smells of paint, glue, and wax, as if the floors have just been polished. All the furniture, baskets, suitcases, and bundles have been unloaded and set up in their places—even mother's piano, the rubber plant in its pot, and all my dolls! Our old things seem new, a bit strange and unfamiliar. And now I'll have a big nursery, and Papa will have his own study, and we'll have hot water from the tap in the bathroom! The room next to the nursery goes to Aunt Maria Nikolayevna, Mama's big sister. She moved in with us recently, and I'm a little afraid of her: She has a very severe look. Even Mama seems shy around her. But today, Auntie has changed: She smiles gently and sings to herself. I think the new place will bring us all a great deal of joy!

? →

Irina's doll carriage

← ?

Slippers

Papa's study

Aunt Maria's room

Main entrance

Living room

Aunt Maria Nikolayevna unpacking

Ilya Stepanovich Muromtsev, father, unpacking books

Irina Muromtseva

Trezor

Nanny Nikiforovna (Efrosinia Nikiforovna Shestova) carrying a ficus plant

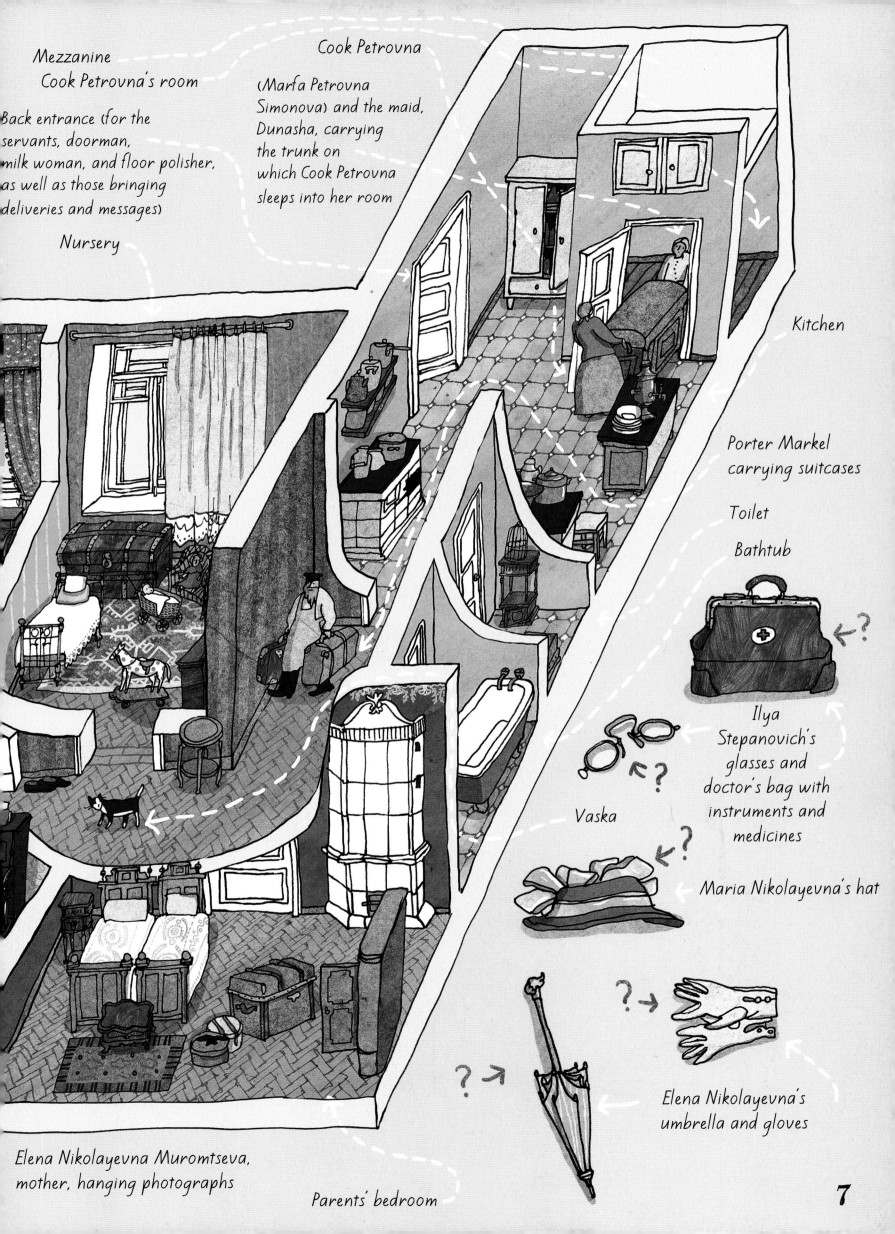

Mezzanine
Cook Petrouna's room

Back entrance (for the servants, doorman, milk woman, and floor polisher, as well as those bringing deliveries and messages)

Nursery

Cook Petrovna

(Marfa Petrovna Simonova) and the maid, Dunasha, carrying the trunk on which Cook Petrovna sleeps into her room

Kitchen

Porter Markel carrying suitcases

Toilet

Bathtub

? ←

Ilya Stepanovich's glasses and doctor's bag with instruments and medicines

? ↙

Vaska

? ←

Maria Nikolayevna's hat

? →

? →

Elena Nikolayevna's umbrella and gloves

Elena Nikolayevna Muromtseva, mother, hanging photographs

Parents' bedroom

7

Nikolai Muromtsev
December 25

1914 Christmas! Delicious smells come from the kitchen, and candles are already lit on the tree we brought yesterday from the market in Theater Square. Snow falls outside the window. We won't have a big children's party this year. Only the two Volkova sisters, Marusya's friends, have come over with their nanny. The nanny went straight to the kitchen to have tea, and Mama sat at the piano, and the girls started singing: "My Lizochek is so small, is so small, is so small." Boring! And all because there's a war and Papa is on the frontlines healing the wounded. It's not a holiday without him. Last year, we played charades and hide-and-seek and a new board game with planes and airships! Then we danced the polka and mazurka, and then Mama played a march loudly and Papa took down toys and gingerbread from the tree and gave them to our guests.

They say the war will be over very soon, and the Germans and Austrians will never get to Paris or Warsaw. The newspapers write that this is the Second Patriotic War, and Germany's Kaiser Wilhelm

ll will end up just like Napoleon. We have to help our heroes as best we can: Mama goes to the workshop to pluck lint to make bandages. Irina signed up for nursing courses, and Marusya and I put all our pocket money into a cup for the Red Cross—a half-ruble, three fifteen-kopek coins, and two rubles. I "arrested" Marusya's big German doll as a spy and wanted to shoot her, but Marusya let out a howl! Nanny came running and took away the doll. But the German spies are everywhere! At the front, and at the capital in St. Petersburg and even here in Moscow! I explained that to Mama, but she said that the doll was innocent and that Mr. Seidler from the Viennese bakery was not a spy but a third-generation Russian citizen who helps the Red Cross.

We were setting the holiday table when the doorbell rang! Who could it be? Nanny answered the door and gasped loudly. There was Papa, coming into the living room in boots and an overcoat!

1914

The war Russia entered on August 1, 1914, would later be called World War I. It encompassed all of Europe and lasted a long four years. It was not only two or three countries that were fighting among themselves, but also allies of those countries. On one side: England, France, and Russia. On the other: Germany and Austria-Hungary. Each side was joined by numerous allies, from Brazil to China! They fought on land, at sea, and even in the air. The armies lost more than ten million people combined, and many civilians were also killed.

German soldiers

Russian soldiers

French soldiers

THERE ARE SO MANY PEOPLE WOUNDED, AND THERE ARE HOSPITALS EVERYWHERE. HOW DO YOU MANAGE?

ILYA, HOW ARE THINGS AT THE FRONT?

IT'S HELL! THERE AREN'T ENOUGH UNIFORMS AND BOOTS. THE SOLDIERS ARE FREEZING IN THE TRENCHES. WE DON'T HAVE ENOUGH MEDICAL SUPPLIES. THE LOSSES ARE ENORMOUS.

IN HARD TIMES, THE MOST IMPORTANT THING IS ECONOMIZING. MAGAZINES ARE PRINTING RECIPES FOR CHEAP MEALS. TODAY, I HAD THE COOK MAKE DRACHENA, A KIND OF CAKE, FOR DESSERT. HERE'S THE RECIPE I COPIED FROM *MODNY SVET (FASHIONABLE WORLD)*.

PAPA, TELL US ABOUT THE WAR!

Irina
Trishka

The money Marusya and Nikolenka gave to help the wounded

Drachena

In a bowl, whip 1/8 lb butter. In another bowl, beat 3 eggs with 1/2 cup sugar. Mix in with the butter and add 1/2 tsp salt and 2 cups flour. Mix together and gradually add in 2 cups milk. Melt 1 tbs of butter in a large frying pan. Pour in dough and cook on a stovetop for about 30 minutes. Serve with jam.

* 1/8 lb of butter equals 4 tbs

Two rubles

Nikolenka
Marusya

Aunt Maria Nikolayevna

Elena Nikolayevna Muromtseva, mother

Ilya Stepanovich Muromtsev, father of Irina, Nikolenka, and Marusya

Airplane

A half-ruble

Efrosinia Nikiforovna, nanny

Newspaper asking for book donations for the soldiers

END THIS WAR! THE PEOPLE DON'T NEED IT. RUSSIAN WORKERS ARE FIGHTING GERMAN WORKERS WHEN THEY SHOULD BE JOINING TOGETHER TO FIGHT THE CAPITALISTS AND THE BLOODTHIRSTY TSAR.

Three fifteen-kopek coins

HOW IS MY GRISHA DOING FIGHTING THE GERMANS?

ЖЕРТВУЙТЕ НА КНИГУ—СОЛДАТУ.

Отъ московскаго мѣстнаго комитета Краснаго Креста снабженія раненыхъ произведеніями печати.

Позиціонный характеръ веденія войны за послѣдній періодъ выдвинулъ самую насущную нужду арміи, какъ солдату, такъ и офицеру нужна книга. Каждый изъ насъ долженъ немедленно принять участіе въ удовлетвореніи духовныхъ запросовъ, защищающихъ нашу родину и насъ.

Длительные часы пребыванія въ окопахъ, жизнь въ землянкахъ, дальность разстоянія отъ культурныхъ центровъ,—все это можетъ быть скрашено книгой.

Комитетъ снабженія раненыхъ произведеніями печати получилъ разрѣшеніе отъ Главнокомандующаго снабдить армію солдатскими и офицерскими библіотеками. Въ своемъ разрѣшеніи Главнокомандующій сообщаетъ, что считаетъ снабженіе

FIRST, WE CHASE OUT THE ENEMY. THEN WE'LL DEAL WITH THE TSAR. TODAY, WE MUST UNITE AND DEFEND OUR HOMELAND.

A SOCIALIST HAS NO HOMELAND!

Sergei Voloshin, Irina's fiancé

Igor, Sergei's friend

Cake

Papa's favorite cup

Crystal sugar bowl holding sugar cubes

Samovar

These are the kinds of desserts that were sold in Mr. Seidler's Viennese pastry shop. How sad that he had shut down the store after the pogrom!

Muff

Gaiters—like thick socks with buttons

Papa's warm felt boots

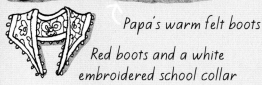

Red boots and a white embroidered school collar

The Volkova sisters

I AM WEARING A SAILOR SHIRT AND SHORTS. LYUBA VOLKOVA IS DRESSED IN THE LATEST FASHION, WEARING THE COLORS OF THE COUNTRIES THAT WERE ALLIED WITH RUSSIA DURING THE WAR.

I SENT A CHRISTMAS CARD TO NATASHA, OUR FRIEND FROM THE COUNTRY HOUSE, AND MARUSYA TEASED ME ABOUT BEING IN LOVE!

Nikolka's letter wishes Natasha "Happy New Year!"

Дорогая Наташа поздравляю тебя съ Н.Г. я провелъ праздники весело и теб желаю такъ-же провести Любящю тебя ... Николай

AT THE WORKSHOP ON ILYINKA STREET, WE PUT TOGETHER UP TO TEN THOUSAND BANDAGE PACKETS EACH DAY.

Toy soldiers

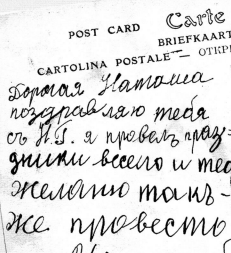

Irina plucking lint to make bandages

The dolls have porcelain heads, hands, and feet, and their bodies are stuffed with sawdust.

Inkwell and three pens

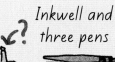

Ink blotter

Doctor's stethoscope

Tree ornaments

Pony on wheels

These are the toys Nikolka and Marusya got for Christmas.

11

Marusya Muromtseva
February 21

1919 This year, Nikolka and I did not go ice-skating or to visit anyone on Epiphany because Mama sees her friends almost every day in "tails," or lines. There are lines waiting for bread, dried fish, and kerosene, as well as lines at the commissary, where you can get cabbage soup with a coupon, and at the housing office, where you can get firewood with a coupon. We got two bundles of firewood for February. We were so careful with it, but we ran out before the month was half over! So we burned all the old magazines and the chairs. Nanny wanted to burn Papa's books, but Mama said they were not to be touched.

Nikolka keeps coughing. He's had a fever for three days. Mama had to run to Samotechnaya Street to get a doctor because she couldn't find a carriage and the trams were not operating. Dr. Ignatov, Father's old friend, came. He shook his head: "Pneumonia. But I can't recommend our hospital—it's chaos there. The wards are full of typhus. And the aides have meetings and rallies every

day, you see. You're better off at home for now." He prescribed milk and broth for Nikolka. Mama and Nanny whispered together, and then they moved the rug. They got out the silver spoons—Mama's dowry—from under it and wrapped them in a rag. In the morning, Mama went to the flea market. Nanny and I hauled up water from the downstairs neighbors—our pipes had burst, but theirs were still holding up. We lit the stove, boiled some water, and made Nikolka carrot tea, and then we waited. It got dark, so we lit the lamp. Comrade Orlik, the man who the Narkompros sent to live with us, came in and went to his room, Papa's former study. Mama came home crying. She had traded the spoons for a piece of horsemeat, but on the way home, she was attacked in the alley by a pack of stray dogs. She dropped the meat and barely got away herself. I was brave and did not cry.

"It's all right, dear," Nanny said. "We'll manage somehow, and before you know it, Ilya Stepanovich will be back."

1919

World War I ended in 1918. Germany was defeated. But even before the end of the war, life in Russia was changed irreversibly. Two revolutions took place in 1917, in February and October. In February, the tsar abdicated and Russia became a republic. The country was to be ruled by a parliament—the Constitutional Assembly—formed by general elections. But the Provisional Government, which had representatives of various parties, postponed the election several times. In November, the Bolshevik Party, headed by Vladimir Lenin, took power.

The Bolsheviks declared Russia a Soviet Republic, with administrators elected from bodies of workers and peasants. Not everyone liked the regime. The Russian Civil War broke out between the Bolsheviks (the Reds) and their opponents (the Whites). But some people took advantage of the chaos to steal and kill without punishment.

Bolshevik poster

ВСЮ ЖИЗНЬ В СУББОТНИК ПРЕВРАТИМ

Newspapers explaining Russia's transition from the Julian calendar to the Gregorian calendar, which is used almost worldwide.

> WE WILL CONQUER COLD, HUNGER, AND DARKNESS. THERE WON'T BE ANY OPPRESSED OR ILLITERATE PEOPLE. WORKERS OF THE WORLD WILL RISE UP, FOLLOWING OUR EXAMPLE.

> COMRADE ORLIK, WHO WILL MANAGE THE BANKS AND FACTORIES?

> THE PROLETARIAT WILL TAKE THINGS INTO THEIR OWN HANDS.

Customary commissar leather jacket Jodhpurs

Comrade Orlik

Comrade Nikitina (Lyalya)

> IN 1918, THE NEW CALENDAR WAS INTRODUCED: FEBRUARY 14 CAME THE DAY AFTER JANUARY 31!

Leon Trotsky A Bolshevik and one of the organizers of the October Revolution. Led the Red Army in 1918. Expelled from the Soviet Union in 1929.

Vladimir Lenin Head of the Bolshevik Party and of the Soviet state. Leader of the October Revolution.

Petya Ostrovsky, an art student studying in Moscow

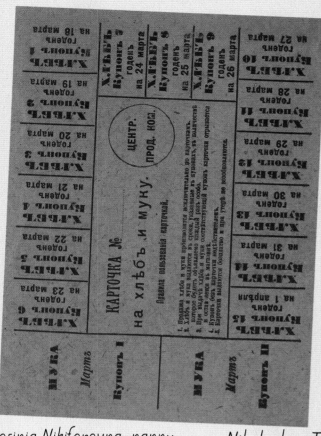

Ration card for bread and flour

The Muromtsevs use their ration cards to get bread and herring and use coupons to get meatless cabbage soup from the commissary. The ration cards are given out by category, and workers get the highest rations. Sometimes, there is nothing left for the non-laboring people.

LET'S TRY TO PICK OUT THE BEST POTATOES.

THEY'RE ALMOST ALL ROTTEN.

WE'LL CUT OUT THE ROTTEN PARTS.

Coarse black bread

Rationed herring

Cabbage

Sprouted potatoes

Efrosinia Nikiforovna, nanny　　Nikolenka　Trishka　　Elena Nikolayevna　　Marusya

TYPHUS IS CONTAGIOUS AND VERY DANGEROUS. THERE IS NO EFFECTIVE MEDICINE FOR IT RIGHT NOW.

The water pipes freeze from the cold, so the family has to carry heavy cans and pails of water from the neighbors' apartment downstairs.

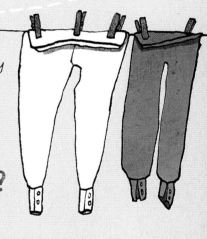

Photograph of Irina and Sergei, which they sent from Rostov, where Sergei joined the White Army

I AM ELENA NIKOLAYEVNA'S FAVORITE POET. IN MAY 1918, SHE BORROWED MY NEW POEM, "THE TWELVE," FROM A FRIEND AND COPIED IT INTO HER NOTEBOOK.

This iron stove is called a burzhuika, which means "little bourgeois." They say it's because the bourgeois, or the capitalist class, don't have firewood for a kitchen stove or ordinary stove anymore. This stove is used to heat the room and for cooking. The burzhuika doesn't need much wood, but it also doesn't provide much heat. When there is no wood, the family burns old books and magazines, furniture, and pickets from fences.

Отъ зданія къ зданію
Протянутъ канатъ.
На канатѣ—плакатъ:
« Вся власть Учредительному Собранію!»
Старушка убивается—плачетъ;
Никакъ не пойметъ, что значитъ,
На что такой плакатъ,
Такой огромный лоскутъ?
Сколько бы вышло портянокъ для ребятъ,
А всякій—раздѣтъ, разутъ...
Старушка, какъ курица,
Кой-какъ перемотнулась черезъ сугробъ.
—Охъ, Матушка-Заступница!
—Охъ, большевики загонятъ въ гробъ!

Aleksandr Blok

Petya Simonov
May 23

1927 What a hassle today! I went to the kitchen to see if there was any food. Mama was doing laundry in there and yelled at me: "Why are you wandering around doing nothing? Sit down with Tonya and do your math homework!" Just then, Madam Orlik strode into the kitchen and started shouting at the doctor's wife for burning her new silk stockings with her Primus stove. "Well, don't hang your stockings over other people's stoves!" Nanny Nikiforovna said. The doctor's wife was silent, and she looked totally miserable. She's a fine lady—teaches Tonya piano—but she can't stand up for herself. If not for Nanny Nikiforovna, Madam Orlik would have ranted a long time. The Muromtsevs used to have the whole place to themselves, but now a few families live here together. Just as I sat down with my exercise book, in came Olga Petukhova and Marusya, the doctor's daughter. They wound up the record player and started whirling and swirling, dancing the tango. At that, old lady Shuiskaya, one of the tenants, looked out from her room.

"What's all that noise?" she asked.

I'm not surprised about Olga, but what's with Marusya?

Sonya Gordon let them have it: "A woman must be e-man-ci-pa-ted! Down with the vestiges of the past! Bourgeois society sees women as goods in a shop window, which is what you are de-mon-stra-ting, Comrade Petukhova, with your depraved dancing. Don't you feel ashamed?"

"No," replied Olga. "On the contrary, I like it very much. As for you, citizen Gordon, you should watch yourself. Certain lovebirds loiter under the windows, talking all night and not letting working people sleep."

Sonya turned red. "How dare you! The comrade and I were discussing the female question in light of Bebel's works!"

"We understand that, sweetheart. I, too, would like some Bebelizing after a hard day!" That was Petukhov trying to support his wife.

What can you do with these inconsiderate people—there's no way you can study around them!

1927

The Bolsheviks won the Russian Civil War in 1922. The government declared that the land, factories, and industrial plants belonged to the people, but in fact, they became state property. Private trade and property were banned as relics of capitalism. The former economy was destroyed. The Bolsheviks began confiscating excess grain from the peasants. In 1922, the harvest was poor, and a terrible famine spread through the country, mostly concentrated in the Volga region in southwestern Russia. Almost five million people died of hunger. People streamed to the cities in search of work. Even people who had supported the new regime joined protests. The Bolsheviks were forced to establish the New Economic Policy (NEP). Once again, private trade and small business were allowed. People who engaged in such business were called NEPmen. Life began to smooth out, but the country was still lagging behind the leading developed countries. Young people were called upon to actively participate in building a new life.

In December 1922, a new state was established—the Union of Soviet Socialist Republics, or USSR. It was made up of several republics: Russia, Ukraine, Belorussia (now Belarus), and the Transcaucasian Republic (later divided into Georgia, Armenia, and Azerbaijan). In 1924, Vladimir Lenin (the leader of the USSR) died, and Joseph Stalin rose to power.

Lenin's Mausoleum

The Muromtsevs' Primus stove

The Simonov Primus stove

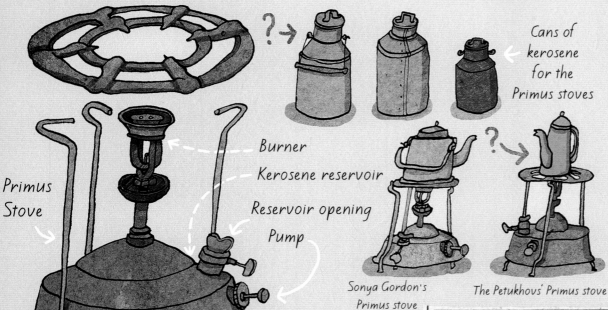

? →

Cans of kerosene for the Primus stoves

Primus Stove

Burner

Kerosene reservoir

Reservoir opening

Pump

Sonya Gordon's Primus stove

The Petukhovs' Primus stove

Now, every family in the apartment has its own Primus stove. The stove make a lot of noise and smoke, and they cook food very slowly. To light one, you have to pump kerosene from its reservoir into its burner and then strike a match over it.

Newspaper advertisement for women's beauty products →

Olga Petukhova

UNDER THE NEP, NEW RICH PEOPLE APPEARED— WE CALLED THEM NEPMEN. EVEN THOUGH IT'S HARD TO SUSTAIN A GOOD ECONOMY WITHOUT PRIVATE TRADE AND MANUFACTURING, EVERYONE HATED THE NEPMEN. PEOPLE THOUGHT THEY WERE VESTIGES OF THE PAST AND MOCKED THEM FOR BEING GREEDY.

Bakelite brooch

Perfume

Necklace

Mascara

Earrings

Powder puff

Powder

Silk undergarments

WHEN I GROW UP, I'LL BE A PILOT!

I WANT TO BE A PILOT, TOO!

YOU'RE A GIRL.

SO WHAT IF SHE'S A GIR

Tonya Simono Petya's sister

Ilyich light bulbs

Kerosene lamp

Vera Pavlovna Shuiskaya

NEW POWER STATIONS ARE BEING BUILT IN THE COUNTRY UNDER THE GOELRO PLAN. THE "ILYICH LAMP" WORKS WELL IN EVERY APARTMENT NOW, BUT THE RESIDENTS KEEP SOME KEROSENE LAMPS AND CANDLES JUST IN CASE.

Petya Simonov

18

WE HAVE BEEN FORCED TO MOVE INTO SMALLER QUARTERS IN OUR OWN APARTMENT SEVERAL TIMES. NOW, THERE ARE SIX DIFFERENT FAMILIES LIVING IN THE APARTMENT. IT IS CROWDED, AND EVERYONE IS UNCOMFORTABLE. IN THE MORNINGS, THERE ARE LONG LINES FOR THE TOILET AND THE BATHROOM, AND SQUABBLES BREAK OUT IN THE KITCHEN ALL DAY LONG. BUT IT'S VERY HARD TO FIND A ROOM IN MOSCOW, SO WE ARE HAPPY TO HAVE THIS PLACE.

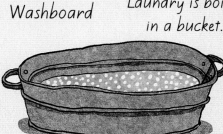

Washboard

Laundry is boiled in a bucket.

The Muromtsevs

Sonya Gordon

Vera Pavlovna Shuiskaya

The Simonovs

Clothes are washed in a tub.

Soap powder   Laundry powder   Iron

The Orliks

The Petukhovs

wspaper advertisements for clothing, tailoring, and jewelry

KLAVA, ARE YOU GOING TO THE LECTURE AT THE CLUB?

NO WAY! MORE TALK ABOUT OPPORTUNISM AND THE LEFTIST OPPOSITION? ZAITSEV INVITED ME TO GO SEE A MOVIE!

В далёкой знойной Аргентине,
Где небо южное так сине,
Там женщины как на картине,
Там Джо влюбился в Кло...

"Last Tango," by Iza Kremer

Pens, notebook, and an inkwell

Textbook

I WORK AS A TRAM CONDUCTOR. AS A REWARD FOR MY HARD WORK, I WAS GIVEN FABRIC FOR A DRESS. IT'S A HIGH-QUALITY TEXTILE.

HOW CAN YOU BE SO OBLIVIOUS! YOU'VE DROPPED ALL YOUR OLD FRIENDS. THAT ZAITSEV IS A BAD INFLUENCE!

NOT AT ALL, SONYA. HE READS ME ESENIN'S POETRY!

Record player

Praskovya Simonova

I AM A PIONEER, A MEMBER OF THE COMMUNIST YOUTH ORGANIZATION. THE KIDS FROM OUR TROOP CREATED AN OUTPOST IN THE COURTYARD WITH THE LIBRARY. WE BROUGHT BOOKS AND A PROJECTOR TO SCREEN MOVIES.

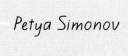

Petya Simonov

Sergei Esenin, a poet

Klava, a friend of Sonya's

Sonya Gordon

Toma Muromtseva
October 12

1937 I woke up during the night because Fedya was crying. It was still dark outside. "You're tormenting the baby again! He's hungry!" Grandmother told Aunt Marusya.

"Elena Nikolayevna, how can you say that?" Uncle Nyuma answered from behind the wardrobe. "You're a cultured woman! Friedrich needs to be fed strictly on schedule."

"Your scientific methods are keeping the girls from getting enough sleep, and then they'll be late for school! Nikolai, why are you quiet? Say something!" Mama said.

While they argued, Fedya kept crying. And then the doorbell rang: two long, one short. That wasn't for us; it was for the neighbors, the Orliks. For my best friend, Iskra. Who would come that late? Maybe the mailman with a telegram? Several pairs of boots walked down the hall and past our door. No, that wasn't a telegram. Maybe comrades from work? Fedya cried even louder. At last, Aunt

Marusya picked him up, and he quieted down. On the other side of the wall, something fell and broke in the Orliks' room. Eventually, I fell asleep. The next morning was normal, but everyone was very quiet for some reason. I didn't finish my porridge, but Mama didn't say anything. Grandfather and Papa didn't argue over who would read the paper first. Uncle Nyuma did his exercises silently. I really like it when he sings loudly in the morning: "My Homeland Is Vast" and "The Happy Wind." You don't need a record player with Uncle Nyuma around! I decided to run to see the neighbors. I wanted to show Iskra my new armband with a red cross, which meant I was now a nurse in our troop. I also wanted to find out who came to visit her family last night. But before I could leave, Grandmother came in. Everyone froze, waiting to hear what she had to say.

"Trouble at the Orliks'. Lev Orlik was arrested."

1937

When the Bolsheviks came to power, they hoped that there would be revolutions all over the world and that popular governments would rise up. Gradually, it became clear that this new world would have to be built only in the USSR. Industrialization began in 1928: large-scale construction of plants to manufacture machines, tractors, and weapons. A five-year development plan was created. It required enormous efforts to fulfill it, and the shock workers initiative started—workers pledged to fulfill and overfulfill the plan by any means.

Peasants were forced to join *kolkhozes*, collective farms, which had to turn over almost all their produce to the state. Those who wanted to continue working the land on their own were branded "kulaks." Their property was taken away, and they were sent to Siberia, a very cold and desolate area that comprised much of the eastern part of the USSR. In 1931, famine returned in Ukraine and the Volga region, and many peasants once again moved to the cities in search of work.

Mistakes and failures were explained as the work of spies. Most of the "spies" were actually innocent citizens forced to confess to trumped-up charges. They were "found" everywhere, arrested, and then they were executed or sent to the camps, where they had to make amends for their "guilt" with unbearable work.

In 1934, Sergei Kirov, a high-ranking Communist leader, was assassinated. Joseph Stalin claimed that this was part of a vast conspiracy to assassinate Soviet leaders and began an intense campaign, known as the Great Purge, to root out and kill the conspirators. This eliminated many people who were politically opposed to Stalin's rule and many innocent people who were forced to admit to crimes they didn't commit.

Emblem of the USSR

The Worker and Kolkhoz Woman stamp from Nikolai's collection

In 1937, the USSR took part the World's Fair in Paris an received many awards. The Soviet pavilion featured the Worker and Kolkhoz Woma sculpture by Vera Mukhina

Lida's Pioneer tie clip reads "Always ready!"

IT MUST BE A MISTAKE. I'VE KNOWN LEV ORLIK FOR A LONG TIME. HE'S A DECENT MAN.

PEOPLE DON'T GET ARRESTED FOR NOTHING. IF IT'S A MISTAKE, THEY'LL FIGURE IT OUT AND LET HIM GO.

WHAT DO YOU MEAN BY DECENT MAN? ILYA STEPANOVICH, YOU ARE POLITICALLY NEARSIGHTED. DON'T YOU READ THE PAPERS? THESE DAYS, YOU HAVE TO BE VIGILANT: THERE COULD BE SPIES AND SABOTEURS ANYWHERE.

Veniamin (Nyuma) Shtein, Marusya's husband

Nelli Muromtseva, Nikolai's wife

Ilya Stepanovich Muromtsev, father of Irina, Nikolai, and Marusya

Mashka

Nikolai Muromtsev, father of Toma and Lida

Metro tokens

I'M AN ENGINEER, AND I WORK ON THE CONSTRUCTION OF THE MOSCOW METRO. I KEPT SOME TOKENS AS A SOUVENIR OF THE OPENING OF THE FIRST METRO LINE IN 1935.

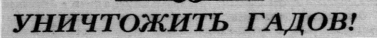

УНИЧТОЖИТЬ ГАДОВ!

Schoolchildren wrote letters to the newspaper expressing outrage at Leon Trotsky's betrayal of Joseph Stalin—and call for Trotsky and his co-conspirators to be punished.

★
Фашистские гадины покушались на жизнь самого родного нам человека, на жизнь нашего отца, вождя и учителя — товарища Сталина.
Враги просчитались. Их поймали с поличным.
Фашиста Троцкого и его сообщников нужно стереть с лица земли — это единодушное мнение всех участников нашего митинга.
Пионеры: ВОЛОДЯ НАУМЕНКО, ВАЛЯ МОСКАЛЕНКО, ОЛЯ ГРИНЕВИЧ.
Киев, 80-я школа.

★
Подлая шайка фашистских наймитов пыталась поднять свою грязную руку на вождей нашей партии и правительства, руку, которая уже обагрена кровью Сергея Мироновича Кирова. Но враги просчитались. Их во-время разоблачил наш славный Народный комиссариат внутренних дел.
Мы, ученики 5-го класса «Г», все, как один, требуем расстрелять фашистских гадин. Подлым убийцам нет места на советской земле!
СЛЕДУЕТ 32 ПОДПИСИ.
Москва, 76-я школа.

Мы, комсомольцы и пионеры 8-го класса «Б» 186-й школы Москвы, возмущены омерзительными, подлейшими преступлениями троцкистских бандитов.
Эти подлые изменники хотели продать нашу родину германскому и японскому фашизму, обречь нас, детей, на голод и холод. Нет слов, чтобы выразить негодование, которым мы охвачены.
Мы хотим, чтобы наш пролетарский суд присудил эту озверелую банду к высшей мере наказания — расстрелу.
СЛЕДУЕТ 16 ПОДПИСЕЙ.
★

★
Жалкие последыши Иудушки Троцкого пытались подорвать военную мощь нашей могучей родины. Они пытались отнять у нас радостное и счастливое детство, которое дали нам коммунистическая партия, любимый Сталин.
Мы требуем расстрелять подлых наемников фашизма.
БОРИС ПЕСЬЯУКОВ.
Воронеж,
2-я полная средняя школа.
★

LIDA, I'VE MEMORIZED IT ALREADY!

NO, LET'S REPEAT IT ONE MORE TIME.

ONLY THOSE WHO LOVE TO WORK GET TO BE LITTLE OCTOBRISTS!

Joseph Stalin
Stalin headed the Bolshevik Party after Lenin's death. The newspapers and radio kept saying: "Despite the deviousness of our enemies, the work of Lenin and Stalin will live forever, and all achievements and victories are possible thanks to our wise leader."

На дубу зелёном,
Да над тем простором
Два сокола ясных
Вели разговоры.

А соколов этих
Люди все узнали:
Первый сокол — Ленин,
Второй сокол — Сталин.

Ой как первый сокол
Со вторым прощался,
Он с предсмертным словом
К другу обращался:

«Сокол ты мой сизый,
Час пришёл расстаться,
Все труды, заботы
На тебя ложатся».

А другой ответил:
«Позабудь тревоги,
Мы тебе кланёмся:—
Не свернём с дороги.

И сдержал он клятву,
Клятву боевую,
Сделал он счастливой
Всю страну родную.

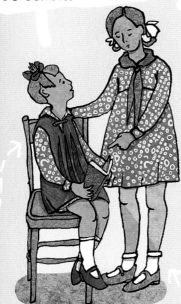

Toma and Lida's toys

Friedrich's bear

Iskra's toys

"Two Falcons," by Mikhail Isakovsky

The Orliks' radio

Toma Muromtseva

Lida Muromtseva, Toma's sister

Lev Orlik's books

Collected works of Karl Marx and Friedrich Engels

Collected works of Vladimir Lenin

AFTER LEV'S ARREST, I WENT THROUGH OUR PHOTO ALBUMS AND CUT OUT THE FACES OF OUR FRIENDS WHO HAD BEEN ARRESTED.

TWO WEEKS AFTER PAPA'S ARREST, MAMA WAS ALSO TAKEN AWAY. AUNT ANYA, PAPA'S SISTER, TOOK ME IN. PAPA WAS SENTENCED TO TEN YEARS WITH NO CORRESPONDENCE—WHICH MEANT EXECUTION. MAMA RETURNED FROM THE CAMPS IN 1946, BUT SHE WAS NOT ALLOWED TO LIVE IN MOSCOW. IN 1956, MY PARENTS WERE REHABILITATED: THE COURT DECLARED THEM COMPLETELY INNOCENT.

Nyuma's badges

Prepared for Anti-Aircraft and Anti-Chemical Weapon Defense

International Organization of Aiding Revolutionaries

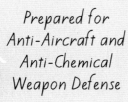

Society for Cooperation with Defense, Aviation, and Chemical Industry

Iskra Orlik

Lyalya Orlik, Iskra's mother

Toma Muromtseva
December 31

1941 When I write to Papa, who is at the battlefront, I always start with good news. I don't want him to worry, and I want him to know that we're fighting, too! Our troop, named for Rosa Luxemburg, collected the most bottles. Lida is working at the factory making shells. Aunt Marusya is not just a teacher; she's the principal at a school in Ulyanovsk. Mama came back home after digging trenches around Moscow and is working in a hospital. The best, most important good news is that the fascists were chased away from Moscow! I sign the letter: "With a Pioneer salute, Toma."

Every night, after Grandmother closes the blackout shades and lights the lamp, the apartment seems particularly empty and echoey. But I don't write to Papa about that. The only residents left are Lida, Mama, Grandmother, Grandfather, and me. And the Simonovs—Praskovya and Tonya—but

they leave early and come back late, so I almost never see them. Old lady Shuiskaya used to live with us, but she died last month. She was afraid of the air raids, and Grandfather said her heart couldn't take the strain. The rest of the people who used to live here are either being evacuated or they are at the front.

So, this New Year's Eve, we are alone in the apartment. Grandmother found a big fir branch somewhere. Lida and I decorated it and put the Soviet star, with the hammer and sickle in the center, on top. We found a candle, cut it up into small pieces, and lit them. Grandfather poured each of us a drink and made a formal toast: "Well, my girls, let's drink to victory! So that in the New Year, the Red Army destroys the enemy!" Lida and I shouted "Hurrah!" and Mama burst into tears.

Fedya Shtein
May 9

1945 Victory! The war is over! Toma and Lida ran to Red Square, and I went with them. Everyone there was hugging, crying, laughing, and singing. Girls were dancing with one another to accordion music, and people were using blankets to toss soldiers up in the air! They raised an enormous portrait of Stalin on a dirigible, and in the evening, there were fireworks—world class! And we had a party in the kitchen.

We all shared two jars of potted meat, and each got a piece of buttered bread. White bread! Toma made Sergo dance with her—he's the one-legged lieutenant the government moved into our kitchen storeroom. Grandmother hugged Aunt Nelli. They really hate each other, but they stood together and wept. I kept waiting for the door to open and for Papa to come in. When I was younger, I didn't understand anything: When Mama would say, "Now, when the war is over, our papa and Nikolka will

come back, and then . . ." I would ask, "Will Grandfather come back, too?" Now I'm a big boy, and I know that Grandfather died and we will never see him again. But Papa is alive. He heals our soldiers, and he writes me letters: "Friedrich, take care of Mama. Listen to her and Grandmother. Study hard." I looked at a prewar photo with the three of us. Mama is in a white dress, holding me in her arms, and I'm a fat, bald baby. Papa is also in the photo. He's tall with curly hair, and he's wearing a striped T-shirt. I thought I would be able to recognize him when he came home because of the photo. And while everyone was celebrating the victory, clinking glasses, dancing, crying, and singing songs, I kept waiting for Papa. Finally, the doorbell rang, and I ran to answer—and there was some woman I didn't know in a uniform. Mama and Lida hugged her hard: "Sonya! Sonechka!" Mama said she was our neighbor, "before the war." I don't remember her at all. Papa didn't come home that day.

1941-1945

For a long time, the Soviets were a threat to many countries. But in the 1930s, a new threat appeared in Europe when the Nazis, headed by Adolf Hitler, came to power in Germany. On September 1, 1939, the German army invaded Poland, and World War II began. Germany's allies were Italy, Spain, and Japan. Britain headed the anti-Hitler coalition. Stalin made a non-aggression pact with Hitler, which meant Russia and Germany agreed not to attack each other. But there was also a secret protocol about dividing spheres of interest in Europe. This meant adding several Eastern European countries to the USSR. Lithuania, Latvia, Estonia, and Moldova became Soviet republics in 1940.

Despite the pact, on June 22, 1941, Germany attacked the USSR. For the first months of the war, the Red Army was forced to retreat. In late 1941, the Germans were outside Moscow, and Leningrad was blockaded. Most of the country was under German occupation. The occupiers considered the vanquished people to be second-class citizens and wanted to destroy them—and many civilians were viciously killed.

From the first days of the war, even "civilian" factories started making weapons. Women and children worked at the factories and plants, and many people volunteered to fight at the front. Despite great losses, a breakthrough occurred in the war thanks to the heroism of the soldiers and the selfless work on the home front. In the winter of 1942, the Russians defeated the Germans outside Moscow, and in 1943, they prevailed at the Battle of Stalingrad. After this, the Red Army went on the attack. The United States and the USSR had once been enemies, but now, they united against a common foe: the Germans and their allies. The United States helped the USSR with technology and food supplies. In 1944, the Second Front was opened in Western Europe when the US invaded Normandy, France, which was occupied by the Germans. This meant that the German army had to fight on several major fronts at once, splitting their forces. The Red Army liberated the territory that the Germans held in the USSR and continued chasing the fascists all the way to Berlin, in eastern Germany. The Germans formally surrendered on May 9, 1945. Now the Russian people who had survived sorrow, fear, and starvation had to raise their country up from ruins.

Soviet T-34 tank

Lida Muromtseva assembling shells at a plant

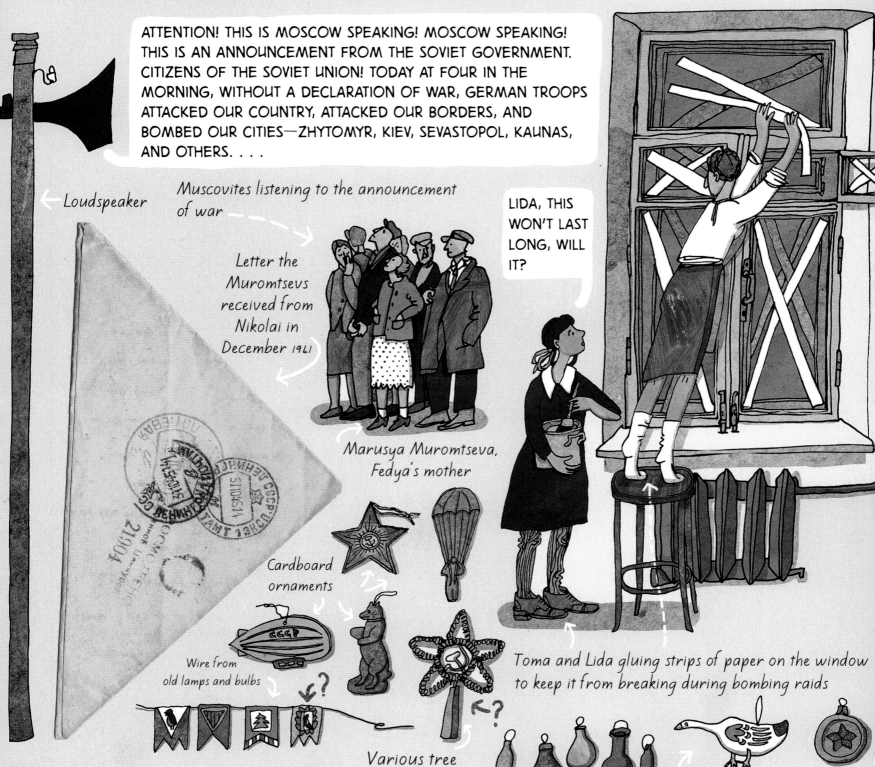

ATTENTION! THIS IS MOSCOW SPEAKING! MOSCOW SPEAKING! THIS IS AN ANNOUNCEMENT FROM THE SOVIET GOVERNMENT. CITIZENS OF THE SOVIET UNION! TODAY AT FOUR IN THE MORNING, WITHOUT A DECLARATION OF WAR, GERMAN TROOPS ATTACKED OUR COUNTRY, ATTACKED OUR BORDERS, AND BOMBED OUR CITIES—ZHYTOMYR, KIEV, SEVASTOPOL, KAUNAS, AND OTHERS. . . .

← Loudspeaker

Muscovites listening to the announcement of war

Letter the Muromtsevs received from Nikolai in December 1941

LIDA, THIS WON'T LAST LONG, WILL IT?

Marusya Muromtseva, Fedya's mother

Cardboard ornaments

Wire from old lamps and bulbs

Toma and Lida gluing strips of paper on the window to keep it from breaking during bombing raids

Various tree ornaments

Cotton bird

Glass star

28

ON THE MORNING OF JUNE 2, 1941, I IMMEDIATELY WENT TO SIGN UP FOR THE ARMY, BUT THEY REJECTED ME. I RECEIVED A DRAFT LETTER IN AUGUST. I WAS KILLED NEAR TULA ON NOVEMBER 21, 1941.

IN THE SPRING OF 1942, I WENT BACK TO WORK IN THE CLINIC, BECAUSE MOSCOW NEEDED DOCTORS. ON APRIL 19, 1942, I DIDN'T GET TO THE BOMB SHELTER IN TIME. I WAS KILLED BY SHRAPNEL FROM A BOMB NOT FAR FROM HOME.

I WAS GIVEN "DEFERMENT" AS A SPECIALIST, BUT I VOLUNTEERED IN OCTOBER 1941. I WAS KILLED AT STALINGRAD IN DECEMBER 1942, BUT MY FAMILY WAS TOLD I WAS MISSING, AND THEY KEPT WAITING FOR ME FOR A LONG TIME.

Cookies baked by Grandmother Elena Nikolayevna

Socks and mittens knit by Lida

Handkerchiefs

Footwraps

Salo

Soap

Book

Tea

A drawstring bag embroidered by Toma

dhpurs
otwraps

Petya Simonov, soldier

Ilya Stepanovich Muromtsev, Nikolai's father

Nikolai Muromtsev, father of Toma and Lida, militia soldier

Wooden crate used by the family to ship gifts to Nikolai

WHEN THE WAR STARTED, I WAS SENT TO A TANK SCHOOL. SIX MONTHS LATER, OUR CLASS WAS SENT TO THE FRONT. I BURNED TO DEATH IN A TANK NEAR KURSK ON JULY 6, 1943.

I REACHED BERLIN AND WAS BADLY WOUNDED IN THE FINAL DAYS OF THE WAR. ON APRIL 28, 1945, I DIED IN THE HOSPITAL.

WE WERE LIVING IN MINSK WHEN THE WAR STARTED. THERE WAS NO WAY WE COULD GET OUT. ON JUNE 28, THE GERMANS WERE ALREADY IN THE CITY. ON NOVEMBER 7, 1941, WE WERE SHOT ON A GHETTO STREET DURING A RAID.

ATTENTION! MOSCOW SPEAKING! ON MAY 8, 1945, IN BERLIN, THE GERMANS SURRENDERED. THE GREAT PATRIOTIC WAR, FOUGHT BY THE SOVIET PEOPLE AGAINST THE GERMAN FASCIST INVADERS, HAS ENDED VICTORIOUSLY! GERMANY IS DEFEATED! WE WILL FOREVER REMEMBER THE HEROES WHO FELL IN COMBAT TO PRESERVE THE FREEDOM AND INDEPENDENCE OF OUR HOMELAND.

Loudspeaker

Mikhail Kotlyar, fiancé of Lida Muromtseva, junior lieutenant

Stepan Simonov, Petya's father, senior sergeant

Abram Naumovich and Ester Girshevna Shtein, Fedya's grandparents

Lena Shtein
March 5

1953 Stalin died today. It was announced on the radio this morning. At school, Anna Nikolayevna burst into tears in the middle of the lesson and ran out of the classroom. The rest of us sat in silence. How can it be? Stalin is our beloved leader. He is a friend to Soviet children. He lies awake at night in the Kremlin, thinking about us. How can he die? In the evening, we all gathered in the big room. Sad music played on the radio. It was quiet next door. Our neighbor Vera Apse was not clacking on the sewing machine—how could you work on a day like today?! Friedrich, my older brother, was chosen to be in the honor guard in front of the portrait of the leader at his boys' school. They chose him because he is an honor student and belongs to the Komsomol. He spent the evening at home and didn't even go over to Borya Apse's to play chess—because how can you think about chess at a time like this?

"What will happen now?" Aunt Lida kept crying and repeating, "How can we live without him?"

"If we don't have this one, there will be another," said Mama.

Aunt Lida hushed her and said, "Are you crazy?! The neighbors will hear you!"

Uncle Sergo came back from the shop and went straight to his room behind the wardrobes. He dropped something on the floor and swore. He must have met up with an old veteran of his regiment again. Aunt Toma and I made dinner and set the table. We were all waiting for Papa. He gets home late now, because he works in a hospital far out of town. Mama says it's only temporary until things clear up. What things? She set out the school workbooks to grade, but she didn't even look at them.

At last, Papa came home. He didn't just come home, he ran in! He stood still, catching his breath, and then threw the radio on the floor. "What are you all bawling about? Do you know how many people he killed?!"

1953

The war-ravaged country was being restored. Many people hoped that life would be freer, but the Cold War, an ideological and economic confrontation between Communism and capitalism, had begun in 1946. (Americans believe it began after World War II.) In the late 1940s, Stalinist repressions began again. "Antipatriotic cosmopolitans" who "bowed to the West" were persecuted. Well-known doctors who treated the Communist Party leadership were accused of being spies and terrorists. The turning point was March 5, 1953, when Joseph Stalin died. The campaign known as the "Doctors' Plot" was immediately stopped, and all those who had been arrested were fully rehabilitated—their names were cleared. Nikita Khrushchev won the power struggle that followed Stalin's death. The beginning of his administration was called the Thaw. At the Twentieth Congress of the Soviet Communist Party (a meeting of the Communist Party leaders) in 1956, Stalin's cult of personality was condemned, and victims of the Stalinist repression were released and rehabilitated. Many issues could once again be discussed in public.

But the Cold War continued. After 1945, many of the Eastern European countries liberated by the Red Army at the end of World War II "chose" the socialist path of development, like the USSR, instead of the capitalist path of the West. Those who did not want to follow it were forced, as Hungary was in 1956.

Crowd at Stalin's funeral

Newspaper headline warning of spies who disguised themselves as doctors and professors

ПОДЛЫЕ ШПИОНЫ И УБИЙЦЫ ПОД МАСКОЙ ПРОФЕССОРОВ-ВРАЧЕЙ

POISONERS ARE EVERYWHERE! ONE CITIZEN TOLD ME SHE BROUGHT HOME PILLS FROM THE PHARMACY. SHE BROKE ONE IN HALF, AND THERE WERE TINY WHITE WORMS INSIDE! THE PHARMACIST'S NAME IS KATZ!

HOW CAN THERE BE WORMS IN PILLS, NADIA? THAT'S NONSENSE.

Wool sweater

Croutons

Warm socks

Underpants

Soap

A drawstring bag

Prized doll with a porcelain head

Lena's dolls, made of plastic

ON JANUARY 13, *PRAVDA* PRINTED ARTICLES ABOUT THE DOCTORS' PLOT. THE ACCUSED MEN ALL CONFESSED TO CONSPIRING TO POISON THE LEADERSHIP OF THE COUNTRY, AND ALMOST ALL HAD JEWISH LAST NAMES, LIKE ME. PATIENTS REFUSED TO LET ME TREAT THEM, DEMANDING A DIFFERENT DOCTOR, AND THE EXPOSÉS CONTINUED. AT THE HOSPITAL, PEOPLE SAID VIGILANCE HAD TO BE HEIGHTENED AND THAT ALL THE KILLER DOCTORS SHOULD BE HANGED IN RED SQUARE. I HAD TO LEAVE MY POSITION AT THE HOSPITAL, AND IT WAS HARD FOR ME TO FIND ANOTHER JOB. I KEPT WAITING TO BE ARRESTED— MY BAG WAS PACKED JUST IN CASE. THERE WERE CRAZY RUMORS EVERYWHERE. . . . THEN SUDDENLY ON APRIL 4, *PRAVDA* REPORTED THAT THE DOCTORS WERE INNOCENT!

Nyuma's suitcase is packed and ready in case he is arrested.

Nadia the milk woman delivers milk to the Muromtsevs every morning.

Toma Muromtseva, Marusya's niece

Nyuma Shtein, father of Lena and Fedya

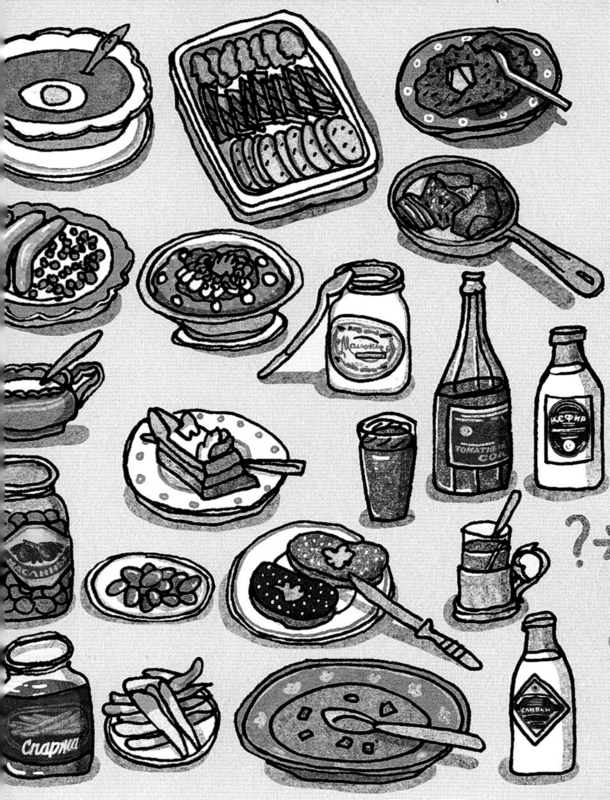

Toma Muromtseva was given The Book of Tasty and Healthy Food. It has recipes for meals for the sick and for children as well as instructions for how to make cream soup or eggplant caviar. It also has information about delicacies that she'd never seen before, such as capers and asparagus.

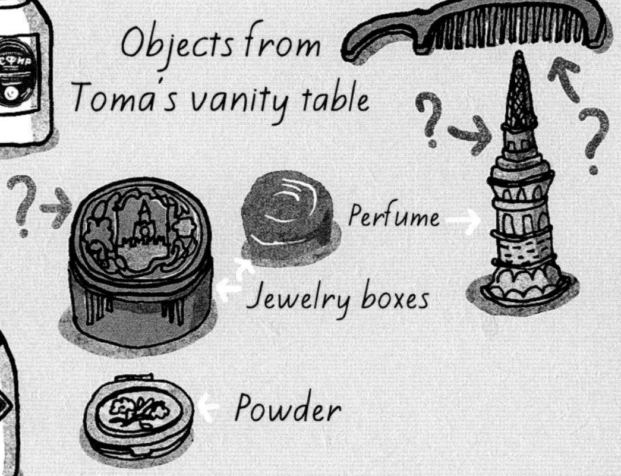

?
?
?

Objects from Toma's vanity table

Perfume

Jewelry boxes

Powder

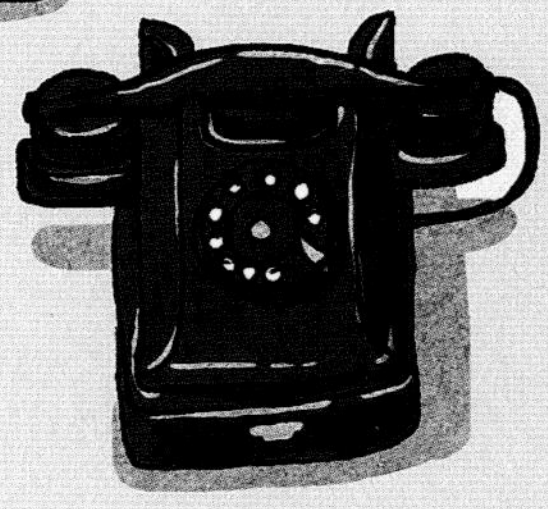

Telephone

In 1953, a telephone was installed in the hallway for all the residents to use.

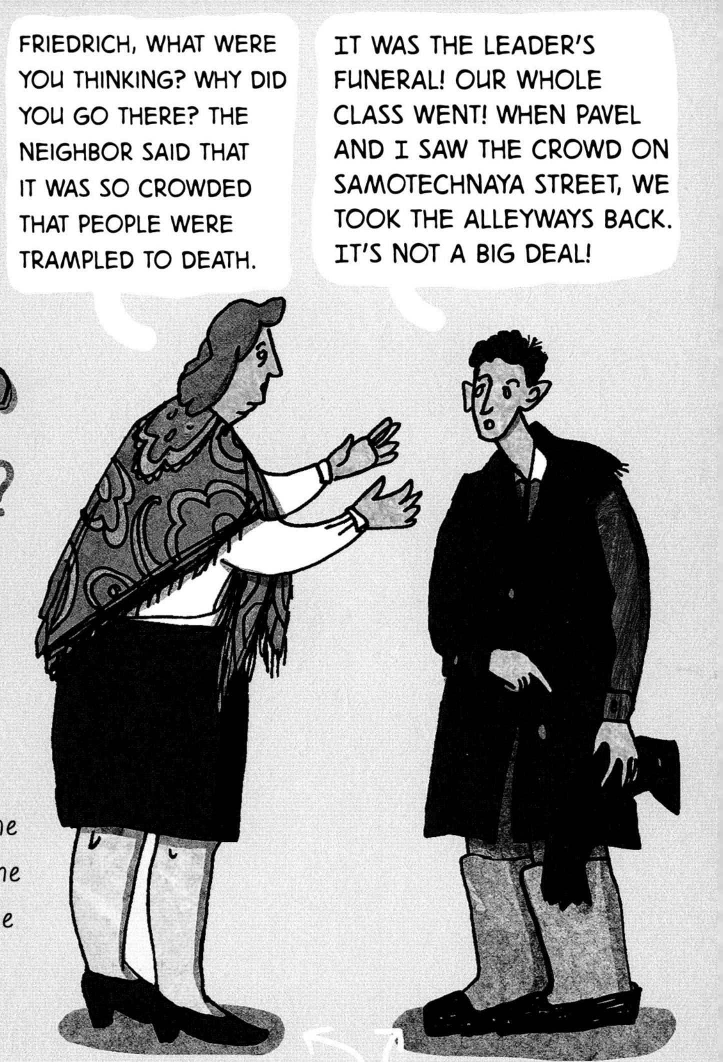

FRIEDRICH, WHAT WERE YOU THINKING? WHY DID YOU GO THERE? THE NEIGHBOR SAID THAT IT WAS SO CROWDED THAT PEOPLE WERE TRAMPLED TO DEATH.
IT WAS THE LEADER'S FUNERAL! OUR WHOLE CLASS WENT! WHEN PAVEL AND I SAW THE CROWD ON SAMOTECHNAYA STREET, WE TOOK THE ALLEYWAYS BACK. IT'S NOT A BIG DEAL!

Marusya Muromtseva, mother of Fedya and Lena

Friedrich (Fedya) Shtein

OTH BOYS AND GIRLS WEAR TOCKINGS, WHICH ARE ATTACHED VITH GARTERS TO UNDERSHIRTS ALLED LIFTERS. THE BOYS' STOCKINGS OFTEN COME UNDONE AND GATHER N FOLDS AT THEIR ANKLES.

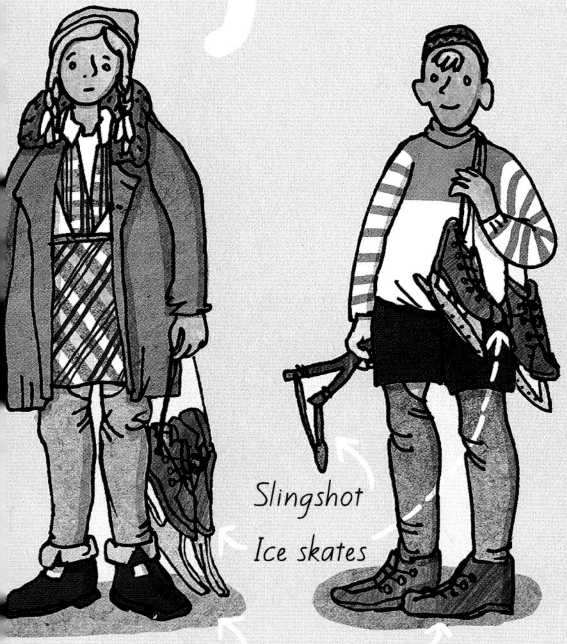

Slingshot

Ice skates

Lena Shtein

Zheka Petrov, Lena's friend

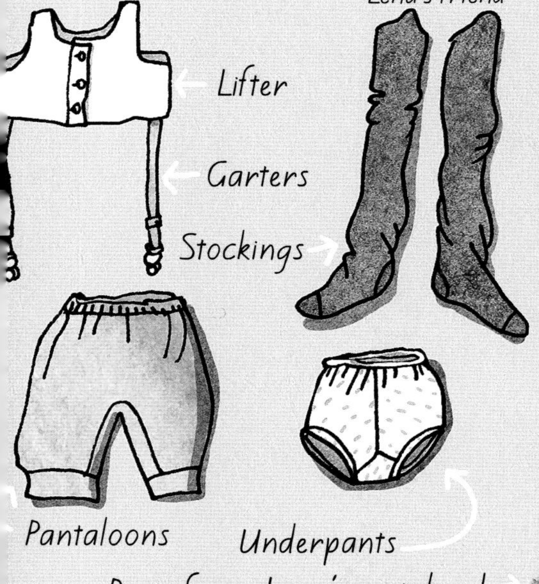

Lifter

Garters

Stockings

Pantaloons

Underpants

Page from Lena's notebook

Report detailing the beginning of the revolution in Petrograd, led by Lenin and Stalin

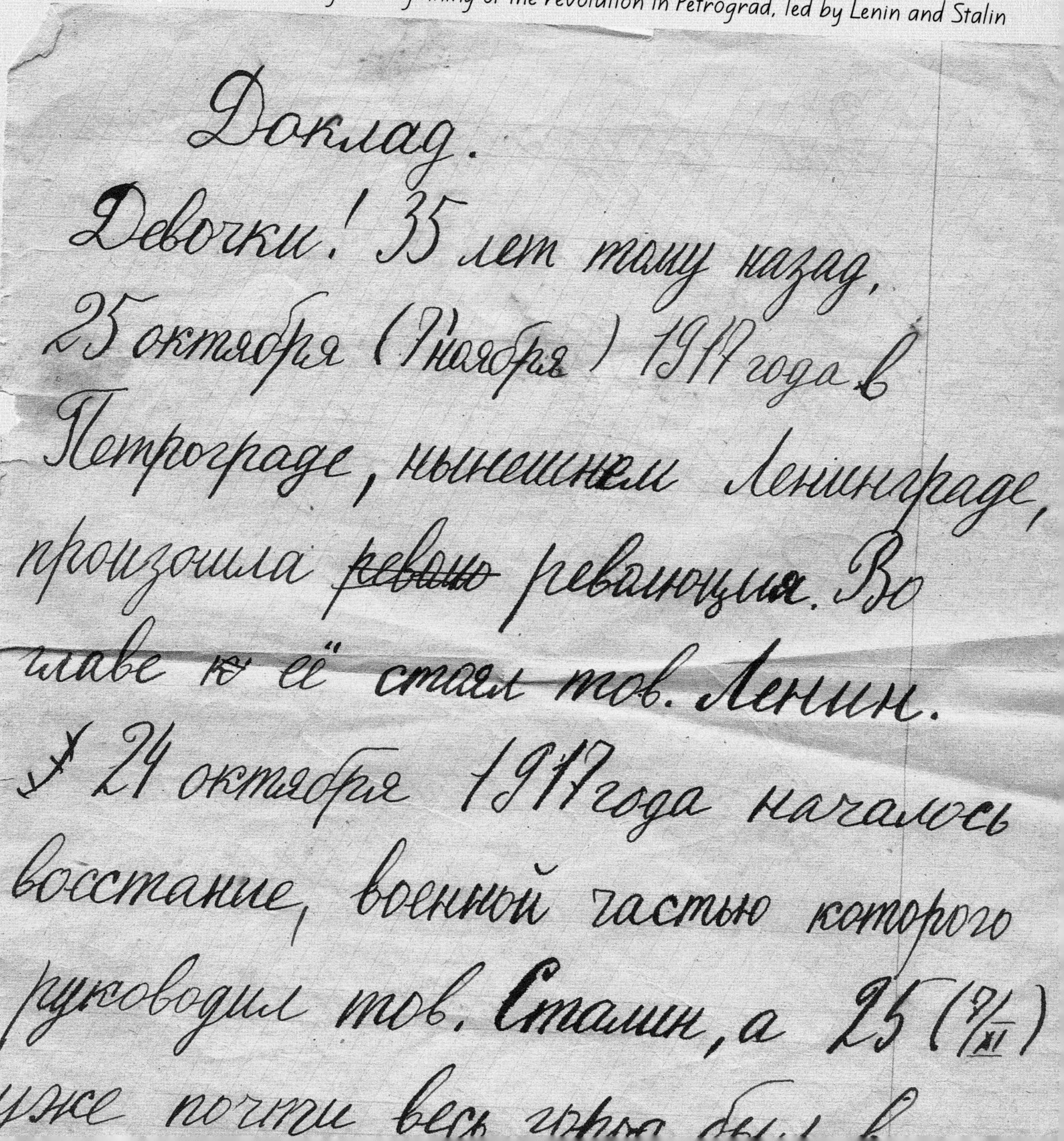

Доклад.

Девочки! 35 лет тому назад,
25 октября (7 ноября) 1917 года в
Петрограде, нынешнем Ленинграде,
произошла ~~револю~~ революция. Во
главе ю её стоял тов. Ленин.
24 октября 1917 года началось
восстание, военной частью которого
руководил тов. Сталин, а 25 (7/XI)
уже почти весь город был в

Genka Muromtsev
April 14

1961

The first man in space is a Soviet! Yuri Gagarin flew in a rocket ship around Earth and came back! Uncle Friedrich got a call from work and was told that the whole department would go to greet the first cosmonaut. Papa drew a big poster: "Moscow—Cosmos! Gagarin—Hurrah!" So, Friday morning, Friedrich and I took the train to the university. Everyone was lined up by department and led to Leninsky Avenue. Springtime, sunshine! Everyone so happy! I had never seen so many people in my life. There were even more than last year, when Mama took me to the May Day demonstration in Red Square.

"We will surpass America. We already have!" someone in the crowd shouted.

"He's coming! He's coming!" someone else yelled.

We weren't in the first row, but Friedrich put me on his shoulders, and I saw everything: Yuri

Gagarin was standing up in a convertible, smiling and waving! Everyone shouted and clapped, but I was the loudest! At the train station, we met Borya Apse, who was also there to greet Gagarin. Friedrich bought me ice cream. Borya and Friedrich wanted a beer, but there was only one kiosk, and the line was long, so we didn't try. That evening, we all gathered in front of the TV to watch the news. They showed Gagarin getting out of a plane and walking down the red carpet to a podium to report on his flight—and his shoelace was untied! Everyone froze. What if he tripped and fell? But he didn't notice. I used to want to be a geologist like Borya: go on expeditions, cook around a campfire, go white-water rafting, look for oil or diamonds or rare metals. But now, I know for sure: When I grow up, I'm going to be a cosmonaut.

1961

The Thaw went on. After criticism of past mistakes by the Communist Party and Stalin himself, the USSR continued along the path to its projected radiant socialist future. The Communist Party was still in charge. Nikita Khrushchev announced: "This generation of Soviet people will live under Communism!" After Yuri Gagarin became the first man in space, it seemed to the people of the USSR that their country was the best in the world and that the era of universal happiness and prosperity was just around the corner. The lives of the Soviet people improved. Many were moved from communal flats and barracks into individual apartments in new buildings. The stores had more food, clothing, and amazing new technology—televisions, refrigerators, vacuum cleaners. Many of these things were affordable for ordinary people. In the meantime, the Cold War reached its peak. The Caribbean Crisis (also known as the Cuban Missile Crisis)—the conflict between the United States and the USSR over Soviet missiles in Cuba—practically led to nuclear war.

"Fierce and Stubborn," by Bulat Okudzhava

Неистов и упрям,
Гори, огонь, гори.
На смену декабрям
Приходят январи.

Нам всё дано сполна—
И радости, и смех,
одна на всех луна,
весна одна на всех.

Прожить лета б дотла,
а там пускай ведут
за все твои дела
На самый страшный суд.

Пусть оправданья нет,
и даже век спустя
семь бед — один ответ,
один ответ — пустяк.

Неистов и упрям,
гори, огонь, гори.
На смену декабрям
приходят январи.

The Apses' record player

Perpetual calendar

Porcelain elephants

HOW COULD YOU BE SILENT WHEN YOUR TEACHERS WERE BEING ATTACKED FOR ELITISM? YOU FOUGHT IN THE WAR! WERE YOU AFRAID?

THE REVOLUTION IS DEAD, AND THE CORPSE STINKS!

NO, THE REVOLUTION IS SICK, AND WE HAVE TO HEL IT. WE HAVE TO RETURN TO LENIN'S PRECEPTS!

I AM A COMMUNIST, I FOUGHT FOR THE SOVIET LAND, I BELIEVED THE PARTY, BELIEVED THE LEADER AND NOW I BELIEVE THE TWENTIETH CONGRESS OF THE SOVIET COMMUNIST PARTY.

WOOF!

Friedrich Shtein

Friedrich's classmates

Kostik Alekhin

Marina Chernovich

Valya Vorontsova

Sergo Ninoshvili, Genka's father

Strelka

The pinafores are white for holidays and black for every day.

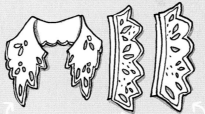

Boys' belt buckle

Genka Muromtsev

Lena Shtein, Genka's aunt

In 1947, school uniforms were introduced in the USSR. The boys wore military tunics and trousers, caps, and belts with buckles. The girls wore brown dresses with aprons.

Collar and cuffs are sewn back on after being washed.

MAMA, LET'S MAKE THE TROUSERS NARROW!

NARROW TROUSERS? NEVER! YOU'RE NOT A *STILYAGA*! VERA, IS THE JACKET TOO LONG?

NO! IT'S THE STYLE NOW: DOUBLE-BREASTED JACKET, NO CUFFS ON THE TROUSERS.

Vera Apse, the seamstress

Newspaper clippings celebrating Soviet technology and space travel

ЧЕЛОВЕК В КОСМОСЕ!

РОШУ ДОЛОЖИТЬ ПАРТИИ И ПРАВИТЕЛЬСТВУ И ЛИЧНО
ИКИТЕ СЕРГЕЕВИЧУ ХРУЩЕВУ, ЧТО ПРИЗЕМЛЕНИЕ
РОШЛО НОРМАЛЬНО, ЧУВСТВУЮ СЕБЯ ХОРОШО

Я ПОБЕДА
НАШЕЙ НАУКИ,
ШЕГО МУЖЕСТВА
УТ КОСМИЧЕСКИЙ КОРАБЛЬ-СПУТНИК
ВЯЩЕННУЮ ЗЕМЛЮ НАШЕЙ РОДИНЫ

ИЗВЕСТИЯ
СОВЕТОВ ДЕПУТАТОВ ТРУДЯЩИХСЯ СССР

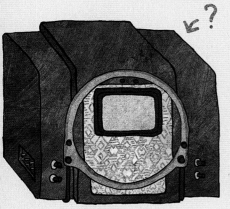

The Muromtsevs' television

In 1956, the Muromtsevs got a miracle of technology—a television. The early models each had a small screen, and you had to attach a special lens to enlarge the image. It was in black and white, and there were only two channels. But soon, color television would come to the USSR.

THIS GENERATION OF SOVIET PEOPLE WILL LIVE UNDER COMMUNISM!

Mug

Bowl

Canned goods

Notebooks
Textbooks

Transistor radio

Folding knife

I AM STUDYING GEOLOGY AT MOSCOW STATE UNIVERSITY. EVERY SUMMER, WE GO ON AN EXPEDITION. THIS YEAR, WE'RE GOING TO THE ALTAI MOUNTAINS. WE WILL RESEARCH MOUNTAIN ORES THERE. HERE'S WHAT I AM TAKING WITH ME.

Sleeping bag

Lantern

Thermos

Borya Apse

David Ninoshvili
August 26

1973

"Gorko! Gorko! It's bitter. Sweeten it with a kiss! *Gorko!"*

Phooey, how much can two people kiss! In front of everyone! That Genka! We've never had a wedding like that in our apartment. Not that it's ever boring: Genka's pals come over. They dance or just listen to loud music until the neighbors start banging on the pipes. He hung a sign on the door to his room that reads: "The best gift is a bottle." Mama was so mad! "Genka, why did you bother with college? To be a hippie? Why don't you just apply for a janitorial job right away?" she asked. But she's wrong: Genka is a good student, even if he doesn't have a Lenin scholarship. And Tanya, his bride, excels in everything. And she's a great skater and skier—they've taken me to the rink with them lots of times.

Half the students from their year at school came, and all of Tanya's family came from the village

of Bezbozhnik. The table was set up across two rooms, and we brought the kitchen stools and borrowed chairs and plates from the neighbors. At one end of the table, someone played the accordion, and on the other, they played Elvis "on bones"—records made out of old X-rays! Uncle Friedrich went off to smoke on the landing with his friends. I snuck behind them, because they chase me away if they notice. "Not for your ears," they always say. Friedrich is living with us for now, because he wants to leave. Forever. Abroad. And the government isn't letting him out. But we're not allowed to talk about that. Or that he types with carbon paper to make copies. I looked at one of the pages, and it said: "Arrests. Illegal political persecution. News in samizdat." I didn't understand a thing. On the stairs, they were whispering about someone named Galich. I'll have to ask Genka. Maybe he'll explain it to me.

1973

The brief Thaw period came to an end. In 1964, Nikita Khrushchev was ousted from power, but the tightening of the screws had already begun. The era of Leonid Brezhnev, who replaced Khrushchev, was known as the Era of Stagnation. But the new generation of Soviet people felt freer. There were those who were prepared to stand up for their beliefs even when they contradicted state policy. In 1968, eight brave men and women came to Red Square to protest the entrance of Soviet troops into Czechoslovakia. Political arguments left the newspapers and entered kitchens. At home, people retyped works that were officially banned and passed them around. They tried to listen to "hostile voices"—Western radio broadcasts—secretly. The USSR seemed completely separated from the rest of the world. This separation became known as the Iron Curtain.

Then suddenly, a loophole appeared for people who wanted to leave the country: You could get permission to reunite with relatives abroad. Sometimes, people had to wait years to get permission. Once they did, they had to say farewell to their homeland and their families.

"Khrushchevka buildings" were constructed to deal with the housing crisis. Marusya and Nyuma, David's great-aunt and -uncle, g[ot] an apartment in one of these buildings.

"Stanzas," by Joseph Brodsky

Стихотворения

ИОСИФА БРОДСКОГО

Е. В., А. Д.

Стансы.

Ни страны, ни погоста
   не хочу выбирать,
На Васильевский остроав
   я приду умирать.
Твой фасад темносиний
   я впотьмах не найду,
между выцветших линий
   на асфальт упаду.

И душа, неустанно
   поспешая во тьму,
промелькнет над мостами
   в петроградском дыму,
и апрельская морось,
   над затылком снежок,
и услышу я голос:
   - До свиданья, дружок.

И увижу две жизни
   далеко за рекой,
к равнодушной отчизне
   прижимаясь щекой,
- словно девочки-сестры
   из непрожитых лет
выбегая на остров
   машут мальчику вслед.

№?
1962

Friedrich Shtein

Sasha, his friend

David Ninoshvili, Genka's brothe[r]

Pushok

Erika typewriter

Carbon paper

VEF 12 radio

The most accessible way to distribute banned texts was by using a typewriter. You could type several copies at once, using carbon paper between the pages. This was called "typing carbon copies." If you hit the keys hard, you coul[d] get several clear copies.

Wedding presents for Genka and Tanya:

Reel-to-reel tape recorder from Genka's parents

...Бродят между разными Добрынями
тунеядцы Несторы и Пимены.
Их имён с эстрад не рассиропили,
В супер их не тискают облаточный:
Эрика берёт четыре копии,
Вот и всё!

...А этого достаточно.

Пусть пока всего четыре копии—
Этого достаточно.

"We're No Worse than Horace," by Aleksandr Galich

Tickets to the Taganka Theatre from Genka and Tanya's classmates

"Madonna" dishes from Tanya's parents

Wine glasses from Genka's grandmother

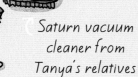
Saturn vacuum cleaner from Tanya's relatives

Embossed metal wall art from Genka's aunt

During the Thaw, new theaters with young actors and a new generation of directors who were not afraid of experimentation appeared in Moscow. Every production at the Sovremennik Theatre or the Taganka Theatre was an event, and getting tickets was almost impossible.

Food at the wedding:

Salads

Fruit

Sausages

Pickles

Plov (a rice and meat dish)

Sausage

Lemon slices

Rock 'n' roll "on bones"
Popular Western music that couldn't be bought in the USSR was recorded on old X-rays in underground studios. This was called music "on bones."

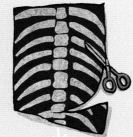

TANYA, LOOK WHAT THE GANG GOT US! TICKETS FOR *THE GOOD PERSON OF SZECHWAN!*

GENKA, WE'LL SEE VYSOTSKY!

Genka Muromtsev and his wife, Tanya

Kombucha (mushroom tea)

THIS FLAT IS COOL! SO ARE THE 'RENTS —NOT LIKE MINE!

YES, THE WEDDING IS GROOVY!

TWIST AND SHOUT!

Headband, called *hair-atnik* (from the English word *hair*)

Bags for documents, called *ksivnik* (from slang *ksiva*, for document)

Bell-bottoms

Oleg and Masha, hippies, classmates of Genka and Tanya

STIERLITZ, PLEASE STAY HERE.

In August 1973, the popular television series *Seventeen Moments of Spring* premiered.

AFTER 1972, I SPENT FOUR YEARS LIVING "IN REFUSAL"—I HAD AN INVITATION FROM RELATIVES IN ISRAEL, BUT I COULD NOT GET PERMISSION TO LEAVE. I WAS FIRED FROM THE RESEARCH INSTITUTE, OF COURSE. I LIVED WITH RELATIVES, DID ODD JOBS, AND STUDIED ENGLISH. SUDDENLY, IN 1976, I WAS ALLOWED TO LEAVE. I FLEW FROM RUSSIA TO VIENNA AND FROM VIENNA TO AMERICA.

Friedrich Shtein

41

August 31

1973

Aleksandr Solzhenitsyn
Writer, dissident, Nobel Prize
laureate (1970). Author of *The
Gulag Archipelago*, a book about
repressions in the USSR. In 1974,
he was charged with treason and
expelled from the country.

Andrei Sakharov
Academic, physicist, one of the creator
of the Soviet hydrogen bomb. He
worked extensively for human rights
in the Soviet Union as an activist and
was awarded the Nobel Peace Prize in
1975. Because of his acts of dissidence,
he was stripped of all his academic
awards and prizes in 1980 and was
exiled from Moscow.

Ravil's toy soldiers

Sonya Gordon
preparing for
a lecture on
Marxism–Leninism

Front door

The Muromtsevs' room

The room that
Genka and
Tanya rent

Friedrich Shtein sleeping
after his night shift

Toma Muromtseva
darning Sergo's socks

Genka and Tanya Muromtsev eating
dinner after returning from their
honeymoon in Jūrmala

David Ninoshvili reading
The Three Musketeers

Strelka sleeping

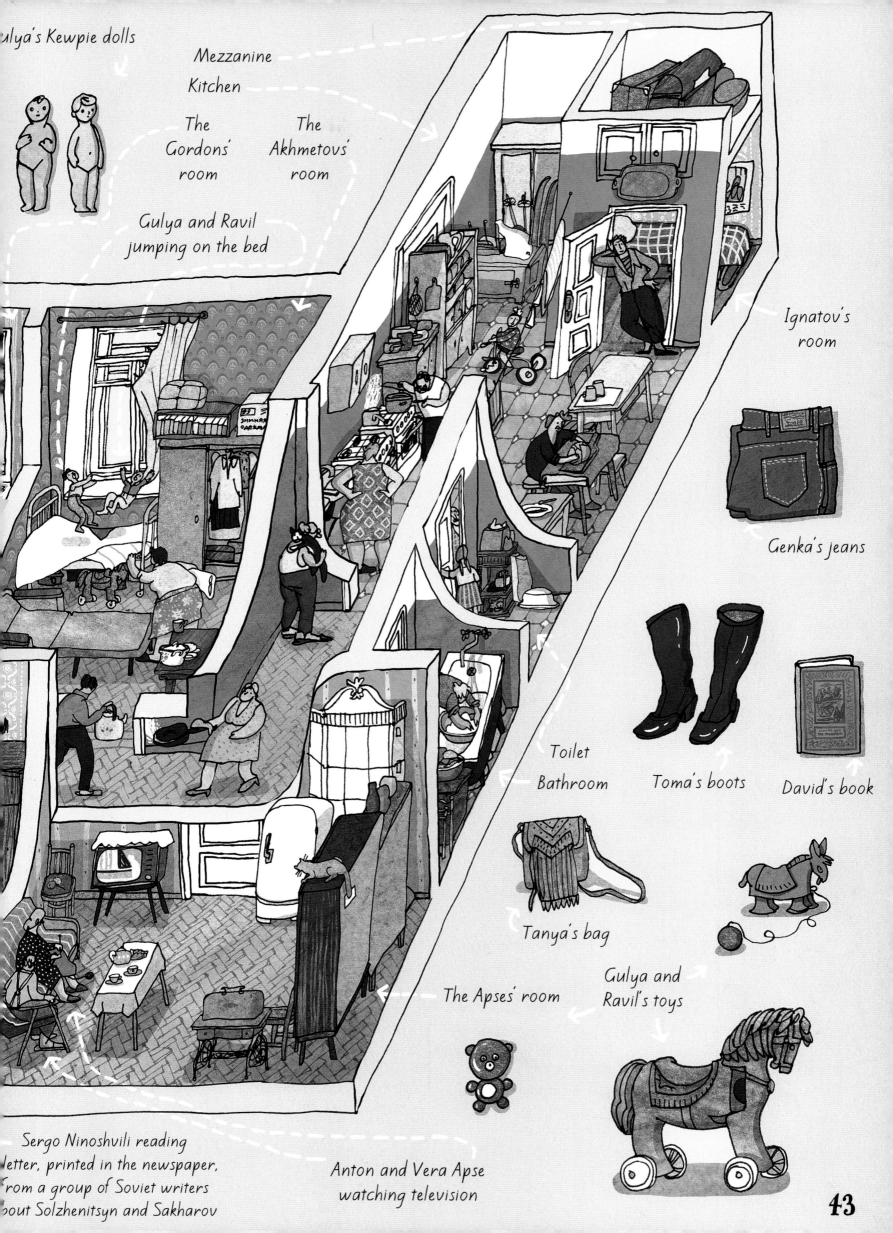

Gulya's Kewpie dolls

Mezzanine
Kitchen

The
Gordons'
room

The
Akhmetovs'
room

Gulya and Ravil
jumping on the bed

Ignatov's
room

Genka's jeans

Toilet
Bathroom

Toma's boots

David's book

Tanya's bag

Gulya and
Ravil's toys

The Apses' room

Sergo Ninoshvili reading
letter, printed in the newspaper,
from a group of Soviet writers
about Solzhenitsyn and Sakharov

Anton and Vera Apse
watching television

43

Sasha Muromtseva
October 29

1987 Great-grandaunt Irina is visiting us—a real Frenchwoman from Paris! I mean, she's actually Russian and speaks Russian, but after her husband—a White Army officer— died in the Russian Civil War, she ended up in Paris and married a Frenchman. Monsieur Dupuy has died. He was a real hero, like Grandfather Sergo. He also fought against the Germans, but in the French Resistance. My great-grandaunt is very old—she must be a hundred, at least—but she's very sprightly and modern—her hairdo is perfect, and she wears high heels. You would never say she was a little old lady. Papa and Mama didn't even know that they had relatives abroad, except for our granduncle Friedrich, who moved to America. But a letter came six months ago. Our parents did not tell us who sent it at first. They whispered with Grandmother and Grandfather, called our grandaunt Lena to come over, and sent Mitka and me out for a walk. Then they announced that our great-grandaunt would be visiting from France and that we could not brag to anyone about it and, in fact, had to keep it quiet. Mama did a major housecleaning

and kept planning what to cook so we wouldn't embarrass ourselves in front of our guest. And so, she came, and everyone gathered here because Great-grandaunt Irina lived in our apartment when she was a girl. She and her sister, Marusya, spent a long time hugging and crying and asking each other: "Do you remember this? Do you?" And then Uncle David pulled out an old suitcase filled with photographs from the kitchen attic. They were prerevolutionary—big, brown, and on cardboard, with the engraved names and addresses of the photo studios: Moscow, Simbirsk, Vilna, Tiflis. And then smaller blurry ones, always with something written on the back: "To Veniamin from Galya as a memory of our friendship!" Some were tiny, like for an ID, and some had lacy edges. Mama got a pencil to write everyone's names. But then Great-grandaunt opened a big bag and handed out presents. Mitka got a T-shirt with the Eiffel Tower on it and some gum, and I got a doll. All her clothes and shoes come off, and her arms bend at the elbows! I'll show all the girls at school tomorrow!

1987

As relations between the USSR and the rest of the world deteriorated, the greatest tension was during the Soviet–Afghan War. From 1979 to 1989, the Soviet Union carried out military operations in Afghanistan, during which tens of thousands of Soviet soldiers and officers were killed or wounded carrying out their "international duty." The country also spent huge amounts of money in an arms race with the West, trying to build the largest military arsenal, and its planned economic growth was stagnant. The leadership of the USSR, headed by Mikhail Gorbachev, decided to start reforms: perestroika, a restructuring of the economy and an acceleration of its development; glasnost, transparency in the press; and détente, a reduction of international tensions. The greatest symbol of this new era was the destruction of the Berlin Wall in 1989. It had been the border between the hostile East and West. (After World War II, Germany was split into two countries, West Germany and East Germany, with West Germany being in the Western orbit and East Germany being in the Soviet orbit. The German city of Berlin was divided between these two countries, and East Berlin and West Berlin were separated by a barrier called the Berlin Wall.) Now reforms were openly discussed on television and in the papers, and real, instead of "official," history was reopened. Books by previously banned authors were published. But the Communist Party was still the only power, and the reforms were controlled from above, because the leaders were afraid things would go too far.

Mikhail Gorbachev

УЧИТЬСЯ ДЕМОКРАТИИ
Партийные комитеты в условиях гласности

хронике наших дней все чаще вс...
...общения такого рода.
...а елгавском заводе «РАФ» посл...
...ого конкурса из числа победит...
...ым голосованием избран новый...

...ве кандидатуры были выдвинуты...
...ого секретаря райкома партии в...
...районе Кемеровской области.
...ома сделал свой выбор путем та...
...вания.
...практику телевидения Грузии...
...ят так называемые «телесходы»...
...ысяч людей. Они приобретают...
...дных референдумов по наиболе...
...ным, волнующим население пр...
...азанные при этом предложения,...
...замечания, рекомендации стано...
...й для принятия важных решени...
...иканском уровне.

Встречи на земле Латвии.

Телефото спец. корр. «Правды» А. Назаре...

Развивать, двигать перестройку
Пребывание М. С. Горбачева в Латви...

Newspaper clippings about government reforms

Presents that Irina brought from Paris:

Vive le français!

T-shirt for Mitya

Tie for Genka (Sasha's father)

Waterproof diapers for Anya

Corn Flakes

Chewing gum

Records for David

Perfume for Marusya (Sasha's great-aunt)

Earrings and pantyhose for Tanya (Sasha's mother)

Candy

Cheese

Art book for Sergo

Doll for Sasha

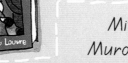
Mitya Muromtsev

> MY GREAT-GREAT-GRANDFATHER WAS A WHITE ARMY OFFICER! JUST LIKE IN THE MOVIES! AND HIS FAMILY LIVED IN LUXURY—WITH A COOK AND A MAID! BUT GRANDMOTHER RAISA'S MOTHER, WHO LIVED IN THE VILLAGE, COULDN'T EVEN GO TO SCHOOL DURING WINTER BEFORE THE REVOLUTION, BECAUSE THEY HAD ONLY THREE PAIRS OF FELT BOOTS FOR TEN CHILDREN.

Novy Mir magazine

The Muromtsevs' bookshelves hold complete editions of the "fat journals" Novy Mir and Inostrannaya Literatura. Novy Mir publish... Boris Pasternak's novel Doctor Zhivago in 1988 for the first time in the USSR, as well as Solzhenitsyn's The Gulag Archipelago. But until just recently, you could be arrested fo... distributing these books!

Mitya and Sasha saved the wrappers from the gum Great-grandaunt Irina brought. Everyone at school was jealous!

MAMA, I'VE BEEN CHRISTENED!

WHAT'S THIS NEW FASHION? WHAT WILL YOUR FATHER SAY?

PAPA'S GRANDFATHER DAVID WAS A PRIEST, YOU KNOW.

David's things:

Bible typed on a typewriter

Small cross

It was widely believed that all citizens of the USSR were atheists. It became evident that this was not true when people were once again free to talk about their religious convictions.

Ох, если бы я умерла
Когда я маленькой была
Тогда б родители мои
Давно имели жигули!

"Oh!", by Natasha Borzhomova

YOU'RE DRESSED LIKE SCARECROWS, SITTING AND LOITERING! WHO'S GOING TO DO ANY WORK?

Жил был художник один
Домик имел и холсты,
Но он актрису любил,
Ту, что любила цветы.
Он тогда продал свой дом,
Продал картины и кров
И на все деньги купил
Целое море цветов.

Lyonya and Nikita, David's friends, punks

THIS IS AN OLD PAINTING, A SELF-PORTRAIT. I CALLED IT "JOB."

OH, I LIKE IT! HOW MUCH DOES IT COST?

"A Million Red Roses," by Andrei Voznesensky

Toma Muromtseva, David's mother

David Ninoshvili, Sasha's uncle

Anya's toys

Sasha's toys

Mitya's toys

Steerable car game

Electronic game ("Just You Wait!")

Efrosinia Nikiforovna, nanny

Elena Nikolayevna, mother

Ilya Stepanovich, father

Sergo Ninoshvili, grandfather of Sasha, Mitya, and Anya

Mr. Smith, an art collector from New York

Marusya

Irina

Nikolenka

Friedrich Shtein

Katya, his wife

Sasha Muromtseva

THAT WINTER SOMEONE BROUGHT US A LETTER FROM FRIEDRICH, A DISTANT RELATIVE WHO LIVES IN AMERICA. HE'S WORKING AS A PROGRAMMER FOR A COMPANY WITH A FUNNY NAME: APPLE! HE ALSO SENT THIS PHOTOGRAPH.

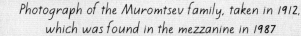

Photograph of the Muromtsev family, taken in 1912, which was found in the mezzanine in 1987

Photo sent by Friedrich from America

47

Anya Muromtseva
August 19

1991

Today is Monday. Mitka, Sasha, and I stayed at the dacha, our country house, while our parents went to Moscow last night. Papa had to be at work in the morning, and Mama had something to do in the city, but she planned to return this evening. She told Mitka to keep an eye on the younger ones (that's us, as if we were babies!). Early in the morning, we heard a roaring rumble, so we ran to the road—and there was a column of tanks. The noise, the dust! Mitka said it was an exercise. We went home, had breakfast, and turned on the radio—and the news announced that a state of emergency had been declared. After the news, they played sad music.

"So, that's the end of perestroika. Pack up, hurry, they may close down the roads, we have to get to Moscow, to our parents," Mitka said.

"Do you think they'll ban the Beatles now?" Sasha asked.

"Anything can happen. Hurry up."

We couldn't call home from the dacha, because we didn't have a phone.

I took my album and pencils and a doll, Sasha stuck her tape player and cassettes in her bag, and we left the dishes unwashed—no time for that. We took the train to Moscow and met Mother on the doorstep—she was planning to come to us. "My smarties," she said. (She didn't know about the dishes or that Mitka had forgotten to lock up the house.)

Grandfather said that the tanks we had seen at the dacha were already in Moscow, and he and Mitka had to go to City Hall. They left. Papa came home from work in the evening, and they were still gone, and there were no calls. What, they couldn't borrow a two-kopek coin from anyone to call us? At last, the phone rang, but it wasn't Mitka with Grandfather, but Grandmother Raisa calling from the train station—she had come from Bezbozhnik with treats for us. She asked Papa to meet her and help her carry the heavy bags. Mama clutched her head, but Grandmother Toma comforted her: "Don't worry, Tanya, whatever happens, pickled tomatoes will be good to have."

1991

Of all the reforms that began in the USSR, glasnost and détente worked the best. Perestroika and the acceleration of the planned economy could not handle the rising prices and the deficits in goods and food. The countries of Eastern Europe and many republics of the USSR sensed the weakening center and decided to break off. The Union republics started declaring their independence, which threatened the territorial unity of the USSR. It felt as if the Cold War was lost and catastrophe loomed in the future. There were men in the Communist Party who wanted to stop the process of collapse and turn back time. On August 19, 1991, they detained Mikhail Gorbachev and declared a state of emergency in the country. Tank troops were brought into Moscow to quell protests. But tens of thousands of Muscovites flooded the streets to defend their freedom, which was symbolized by the White House—the parliament building of the Russian Soviet Federative Socialist Republic (RSFSR) government. They were led by Boris Yeltsin, president of the RSFSR. The attempted coup failed. In December 1991, the Belovezha Accords were signed—the Soviet Union no longer existed, and Russia, Ukraine, and Belorussia formed the Commonwealth of Independent States.

Sergo Ninoshvili, Anya's grandfather, among the protesters at the White House

Newspaper clippings detailing the new Soviet leadership

ЗАЯВЛЕНИЕ СОВЕТСКОГО РУКОВОДС

В связи с невозможностью по состоянию здоровья исполнения Горбачевым Михаилом Сергеевичем обязанностей Президента СССР и переходом в соответствии со статьей 127⁷ Конституции СССР полномочий Президента Союза ССР к вице-президенту СССР Янаеву Геннадию Ивановичу;

в целях преодоления глубокого и всестороннего кризиса, политической, межнациональной и гражданской конфронтации, хаоса и анархии, которые угрожают жизни и безопасности граждан Советского Союза, суверенитету, территориальной целостности, свободе и независимости нашего Отечества;

исходя из результатов всенародного рефе-

рендума о сохранении Союза Советских Социалистических Республик;

руководствуясь жизненно важными интересами народов нашей Родины, всех советских людей,

ЗАЯВЛЯЕМ:

1. В соответствии со статьей 127³ Конституции СССР и статьей 2 Закона СССР «О правовом режиме чрезвычайного положения» и идя навстречу требованиям широких слоев населения о необходимости принятия самых решительных мер по предотвращению сползания общества к общенациональной катастрофе, обеспечения законности и порядка, ввести чрезвычайное положение в отдельных

местностях СССР на срок 6 месяцев с 4 часов по московскому времени 19 августа 1991 года.

2. Установить, что на всей территории СССР безусловное верховенство имеют Конституция СССР и законы Союза ССР.

3. Для управления страной и эффективного осуществления режима чрезвычайного положения образовать Государственный комитет по чрезвычайному положению в СССР (ГКЧП СССР) в следующем составе: Бакланов О. Д.—первый заместитель председателя Совета Обороны СССР, Крючков В. А.—председатель КГБ СССР, Павлов В. С.—премьер-министр СССР, Пуго Б. К.—министр внутренних дел СССР, Стародубцев В. А.—пред-

седатель Крестьянского союза СССР, Тизяков А. И.—президент Ассоциации государственных предприятий и объектов промышленности, строительства, транспорта и связи СССР, Язов Д. Т.—министр обороны СССР, Янаев Г. И.—и. о. Президента СССР.

4. Установить, что решения ГКЧП обязательны для неукоснительного исполнения всеми органами власти и управления, должностными лицами и гражданами на всей территории Союза ССР.

Г. ЯНАЕВ
В. ПАВЛОВ
О. БАКЛАНОВ

18 августа 1991 года.

Во

Some things could be purchased only with ration cards (right)—sugar, for example. Even Genka's new suit required an invitation to buy it in a store—which he got at his job at the research institute—since clothes were also rationed and couldn't be purchased freely.

YOUNG MAN, HOW LONG WILL YOU BE?

ТАКСОФОН

PAPA, I WON'T BE HOME TONIGHT! DON'T WORRY, GRANDPA AND I ARE FINE! WE'RE AT THE WHITE HOUSE. YES, THE TANKS ARE HERE. GRANDPA WENT TO TALK WITH THEIR COMMANDER. SORRY, THERE'S A LINE AT THE PHONE, I HAVE TO RUN. TELL MAMA NOT TO WORRY, OK?

И 5376602 — Крупа или макаронные изделия

И 5376602 — Яйцо столовое или диетическое

"I Want Change," by Victor Tsoi

Перемен! — требуют наши сердца.
Перемен! — требуют наши глаза.
В нашем смехе и в наших слезах,
И в пульсации вен:
«Перемен!
Мы ждём перемен!»

Mitya Muromtsev, Anya's brother

Sasha's cassette player

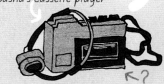

Sonya Krasnova, a student

Л.	Колбасные изделия	сентябрь	Л.	Колбасные изделия	сентябрь	Талон №3
	26943			26943		АХ
	Э1			Э1		8937

Заказ № 7	Заказ № 8
МЫЛО	**Синтетически** моющие средства
III квартал 1990 г.	III квартал 1990

Серия-УТ МУКА сентябрь—октябрь 1991 г.	Серия-УТ МУКА ноябрь—декабрь 1991 г.
Серия-УТ КРУПА (пшено, перловая, ячневая) сентябрь—октябрь 1991 г.	Серия-УТ КРУПА (пшено, перловая, ячневая) ноябрь—декабрь 1991 г.

Примечание. Талоны действительны в указанном периоде. В отдельном виде не принимаются. При утере не возобновляются.

№ 284940

w there are shortages of almost
foods! You can easily buy bread
a can of seaweed, but you have
stock up on pasta and grains
en they appear in the stores. You
ve to stand in line for hours, and
better to go in a group, because
y won't give much to one person.

Tomato juice

Birch juice

Canned seaweed

Khmeli-suneli
spice blend

Vinegar

Bread

Humanitarian aid from
he United States that
Anya's mother was
given at work

Dried bananas
(20 packs)

Cocoa
(1 box)

Rice
(5 boxes)

Spam
(4 cans)

It is not easy to get cheese, so Grandmother
Toma makes it herself. Here is her recipe:
Homemade cheese
Mix 13.5 tbsp (200 ml) of milk and 3.5 tsp
(17.8 ml) of wine vinegar. Stir in 0.03
oz (1 g) of pepsin (you can buy it in a
pharmacy). Strain 10.5 qt (10 L) of milk.
Heat to 86°F (30°C). Add the milk and
vinegar mixture, and put in a warm place
for 30 minutes. Put the pot with milk over a
low flame. Push the curds toward the walls
of the pot.

Newspaper clippings about US President
Bush and USSR President Gorbachev

ращение Президента СССР

чем смысл ввода военных
анки в городе.

In early 1991, 100 rubles was half of Genka's
annual salary at the research institute.
Fashionable Finnish boots cost 120. A year
later, money had been devalued so much
that all you could buy with 100 rubles was
two loaves of bread.

TANYA, HAVE YOU HEARD THAT
THE COMMUNIST PARTY WILL BE
BANNED? *PRAVDA* HASN'T BEEN
PUBLISHED FOR A WEEK!

SASHA, HOW CAN YOU
SAY THAT?! SERGO IS A
COMMUNIST, AND HE'LL
NEVER GIVE UP HIS CARD.

I HOPE THEY GET
RID OF THEM ALL
SOON!

THAT'S TRUE, YOU'LL NEVER
CONVINCE GRANDFATHER
TO CHANGE!

For the start of school
on September 1, the
family bought Anya a uniform and
book bag. But Mama said the
uniform was no longer mandatory.

MAMA, ARE
YOU DONE
YET?

Mitya's
badge

Genka carries goods in bags
like this one

IN LATE 1991, THEY STOPPED PAYING OUR
SALARIES AT THE RESEARCH INSTITUTE
WHERE I WORKED. I HAD TO FEED
THE FAMILY, SO I BECAME A "SHUTTLE
TRADER"—I TRAVELED TO POLAND,
BOUGHT CLOTHING THERE, AND SOLD IT AT
THE CHERKIZOV MARKET. AT FIRST, I WAS
ASHAMED AND EMBARRASSED—I'M AN
ENGINEER; I HAVE A DIPLOMA! BUT THERE
WAS NO OTHER WAY TO MAKE MONEY.

Tanya,
Anya's mother

Genka
Muromtsev,
Anya's father

ha,
a's sister

Murych (the cat)

Toma, Anya's grandmother

Anya Muromtseva

Ilyusha Muromtsev
June 9
2002

Our grandmother is ninety-two years old today! Well, she's technically my great-great-grandaunt Babmusya. We call her that because I couldn't pronounce "Babushka Marusya" when I was little and said "Babmusya." We spent a whole year preparing for this. Mama took Babmusya's address book and called and sent emails to everyone—in France and America, Georgia and Belorussia, Bezbozhnik and Ulyanovsk. So many Muromtsevs everywhere! Mama wanted to invite all of Babmusya's relatives and friends to Moscow. It didn't work well with the friends—some had died and the ones who are still alive are very old and can't travel. But there are lots of relatives—more than we could fit in our one-room apartment. So, Mama decided that we would celebrate in a café, and not just any café, but the one in the apartment where they used to live. They lived in the center of town in a big communal apartment, where they had two rooms. With Grandmother, Grandfather, Great-grandmother, Great-grandfather, and Grandfather's brother, David, and Father's sisters. Then people were moved out of the communal apartment, and it was turned into a café. That's what it's called: "The Old Apartment." Babmusya said it was unrecognizable—they took down the partitions and painted the walls. Only the couch was just like the one they had had. Everyone remembered the apartment except for me and Olya Ninoshvili! Jean-Paul had visited and slept on a cot, and even Aunt Zhenya from America had visited! I felt left out. But they brought out the cake with candles and we all sang: "Happy birthday, Marusya, happy birthday to you!"

Cake with ninety-two candles for Marusya

Zhenya Shtein
Friedrich Shtein
Marusya Muromtseva
Lena Shtein

Ilyusha Muromtsev

Olya Ninoshvili
David Ninoshvili

Jean-Paul Dupuy
Toma
Sergo Ninoshvili

Tanya   Anya   Sonya

Genka   Mitya   Sasha

Anya's cell phone

Sasha's cell phone

Ilyusha's toys

53

WE ARE THE NEIGHBORS, FRIENDS, AND CONTEMPORARIES OF THE MUROMTSEVS. LOOK FOR US BY PAGE NUMBER.

Lev Orlik
1892–1937
(12, 14, 19)

Lyalya Orlik
(Comrade Nikitina)
1900–1968
(12, 14, 17, 19, 20, 23)

Aleksandr Blok
1880–1921
(15)

Markel Ignatov
1862–1941
(7)

Iskra Orlik
1931–2000
(20, 23)

Igor Yaroslavsky
1892–1919
(8, 10)

Sonya (Sonechka) Gordon
1907–1980
(17, 19, 27, 42)

Nadia Trifonova
1910–1969
(32)

Marfa Pavlova
1887–1938
(7)

Olga Petukhova
1897–1972
(16, 18, 19)

Ivan Petukhov
1895–1938
(16, 19)

Aleksandr Solzhenitsyn
1918–2008
(42)

Sakha Gribov
b. 1942
(39, 40)

Zheka Petrov
b. 1945
(33)

Murka
1941–1948
(27)

Gulmira (Gulya) Akhmetova
b. 1968
(43)

Ravil Akhmetov
b. 1967
(43)

Snezhok
1945–1960
(27)

Malysh
1945–1949
(27)

Pushok
1945–1950
(27)

Petya Ostrovsky

1900–1989

(12, 14)

Leon Trotsky

1879–1940

(14)

Vera Pavlovna Shuiskaya

1860–1941

(17, 18, 19)

Vladimir Lenin

1870–1924

(14)

Joseph Stalin

1878–1953

(23)

Lyuba Volkova

1906–1990

(9, 11)

Liza Volkova

1908–1918

(9, 11)

Sergei Esenin

1895–1925

(19)

John Smith

1937–2012

(47)

Oleg Shchurov

1953–1980

(38, 41)

Masha Utkina

b. 1952

(41)

Vera Apse

1920–1997

(26, 31, 35, 37, 43, 49)

Anton Apse

1920–1998

(26, 31, 35)

Valya Vorontsova

b. 1936

(36)

Kostik Alekhin

1937–2015

(36)

Marina Chernovich

1937–2010

(36)

Borya Apse

b. 1938

(26, 31, 35, 37)

Lyonya Demyanov

b. 1961

(47)

Nikita Golubev

b. 1964

(47)

Mikhail Gorbachev

b. 1931

(46)

Andrei Sakharov

1921–1989

(42)

Afterword

They say the past is like a foreign country. But is it? After all, the past is everywhere, and it doesn't vanish. Many objects in our homes preserve our family history. And through the family history, they preserve the country's history. At some point, all children wonder who their grandparents were, how their parents lived when they were little, and what relationships the people in old family photos have to them. The questions, and our replies, represent an important stage of development. Through talking about our personal and family histories, we introduce children to the outside world and explain who we are. There were times in Russia when many events and even members of your own family could not be mentioned. The children from those days now say, "No one ever told me anything about this," and, "We never talked about him or her." And now, it is sometimes hard to bring up these stories. Our book may suggest topics for such a conversation.

There are no secrets in this book. For an entire century, we were welcome guests in the Muromtsev apartment in one of Moscow's old buildings. The country's history is reflected in the family's joys and losses, hopes and disappointments, as it is in the stories and memories of any family that lived in the twentieth century. The songs on the radio, the books, the clothes in the wardrobe, and the meager or abundant fare on the family table are sometimes even more truthful witnesses than the people. You just have to listen to their stories. Which we did, and we passed them along to our readers so we could take a voyage into the past.

THE AUTHOR AND ARTIST EXPRESS ENORMOUS THANKS TO M. O. FILIPPOVA AND E. KOPYLOVA OF THE STATE PUBLIC HISTORICAL LIBRARY OF RUSSIA FOR THEIR HELP ON THIS BOOK.
WE ARE ALSO GRATEFUL FOR THE MATERIAL SUPPLIED BY:
EKATERINA MINOVA,
NATALIA VASILKOVA,
SERGEI KHALIZEV,
TATINA MULYARCHIK,
PETR PASTERNAK,
ANDREI DESNITSKY,
MARINA GRIBANOVA, AND
NINA KUZMINA.

THE ARTIST THANKS ALL HER FOLLOWERS ON FACEBOOK FOR THEIR INVALUABLE HELP IN FINDING MATERIAL FOR THE BOOK.

THE AUTHOR THANKS L. V. SHABSHINA, E. N. KOROTKAYA, AND MIKHAIL ALTSHULLER FOR STORIES, PHOTOGRAPHS, AND UNLIMITED PATIENCE AND SUPPORT, AS WELL AS EKATERINA STEPANENKO FOR HELP ON THE BOOK.

Anna Desnitskaya

Alexandra Litvina

Glossary

abdicate: To voluntarily give up power, especially of a hereditary ruling position.

arms race: A race between countries at odds with each other to build the largest military arsenal.

Battle of Stalingrad, the (1942–1943): A large World War II battle in which Russia successfully prevented Germany from capturing the city of Stalingrad (now called Volgograd).

Bebel, August (1840–1913): A German socialist politician and writer.

Belovezha Accords (1991): An agreement effecting the dissolution of the Soviet Union and the formation of the Commonwealth of Independent States (comprised of Russia, Ukraine, and Belorussia).

Berlin Wall, the: The wall dividing the city of Berlin during the time that it was split between East Germany and West Germany.

billeting: The practice of housing military personnel in private homes by order of the government.

blackout shades: Heavy shades used to prevent enemy aircraft from locating populated areas.

Bloody Sunday (January 22, 1905): Workers march on St. Petersburg to protest the tsar, and soldiers open fire on the procession. This marks the beginning of the Russian Revolution of 1905.

Bolshevik Party: Political party originally led by Vladimir Lenin that eventually became the Communist Party.

bourgeois class: According to Karl Marx, a class of people who hold capitalist values.

Brezhnev, Leonid (1906–1982): Leader of the Soviet Union from 1964 to 1982. During this time, the Soviet military grew extensively, but the country was plagued by the Era of Stagnation.

Brodsky, Joseph (1940–1996): A Russian poet, exiled from the Soviet Union in 1972. He was awarded the Nobel Prize in Literature in 1987 and was the 1991 US Poet Laureate.

burzhuika: A type of iron stove used for heat—literally "little bourgeois."

capitalism: A system of government and economics prioritizing profit and private or corporate ownership of businesses and assets.

Caribbean Crisis (1962): Commonly known as the Cuban Missile Crisis in the United States; a standoff between the US and the Soviet Union over the installation of nuclear missiles in Cuba.

citizen: A word used to address people who weren't members of the Communist party or among its sympathizers in the Soviet Union.

Cold War: An ideological and economic confrontation between Communism and capitalism. Historically, many believe it began around 1947 with the Truman Doctrine, which pledged aid to nations threatened by Soviet expansionism. It ended in 1991, when the Soviet Union collapsed. It is characterized by high tensions between the United States and the USSR (and their respective allies) and the ever-present possibility of a nuclear confrontation between the two sides. The term "cold" is used because there was no large-scale fighting directly between the two sides, but they each supported major regional wars known as proxy wars.

commissar: A Communist party official.

Commonwealth of Independent States: Official partnership between Russia, Ukraine, and Belorussia created by the Belovezha Agreement in 1991. More countries joined in later years.

communism: A system of politics, government, and economics whose ideals consist of a classless society and the collective ownership of goods and property. In the Soviet Union, communism developed from the ideas of Karl Marx.

comrade: A word used to address members of the Communist party and its sympathizers in the Soviet Union.

cosmonaut: A Russian astronaut.

cult of personality: The encouraged excessive admiration and idealizing of a leader, such as Joseph Stalin; the term was popularized after Stalin's death by Nikita Khrushchev.

dacha: A country home.

Doctors' Plot, the: A fabricated conspiracy to murder Soviet leaders, blamed on a group of doctors, many of them Jewish.

drachena: A type of cake.

Engels, Friedrich (1820–1895): A German writer and philosopher who, along with Karl Marx, wrote *The Communist Manifesto* and other foundational communist works.

Era of Stagnation: A period of economic difficulty in the Soviet Union beginning in 1964.

Esenin, Sergei (1895–1925): A Russian poet.

fascism: A political philosophy or regime that has a centralized government with a dictator. It often exalts race or nation over the individual.

February Revolution (February 1917): Rioters looking for food fought with the police and refused to leave the streets. This was the first stage of the Russian Revolution of 1917, in which the Tsarist system is overthrown and Russia becomes a Republic.

footwrap: A rectangular cloth used to wrap the foot in place of socks.

Gagarin, Yuri (1934–1968): The Soviet pilot and cosmonaut who was the first human in space; he successfully orbited Earth in 1961.

gaiters: Leg warmers; in early-twentieth-century Russia, they were like thick socks with buttons.

Galich, Aleksandr (1918–1977): A poet and songwriter whose work protested conditions in the Soviet Union.

garters: Straps to hold up stockings or socks.

ghetto: A crowded and economically disadvantaged area of a city in which a certain minority is forced to live (often Jews).

glasnost: Literally "openness"; a policy of a more transparent government and more freedom of the press in the Soviet Union, beginning in the late 1980s.

GOELRO plan: A government plan crafted in the early 1920s in order to spread electricity throughout the Soviet Union as part of a push for economic restructuring and general modernization.

Gorbachev, Mikhail (b. 1931): President of the Soviet Union from 1990 to 1991, when it was dissolved, in part due to his policies (especially perestroika and glasnost). He was awarded the Nobel Peace Prize in 1990.

gorko: Bitter.

Great Patriotic War, the: A Russian term for the Eastern front of World War II.

Great Purge, the: Also known as the Great Terror. A campaign of political repression meant to purge the Communist party. Launched by Joseph Stalin, it was meant to eliminate any threat to his leadership.

Gregorian calendar: The most common calendar system used throughout the world; a slight adjustment to the Julian calendar. The Soviet Union adopted the Gregorian calendar (new style) in 1918.

hammer and sickle: A Communist emblem that appeared extensively throughout the Soviet Union and on the Soviet flag. The sickle (a type of farm tool) stood for peasants, and the hammer stood for the workers in the industrial sector—the two symbols together represented the unification of these two parts of the labor force as the working class.

Ilyich lamp: Light with a bare bulb that from the ceiling.

Iron Curtain: The metaphorical name for the division between the Eastern bloc and the Western world.

jodhpurs: Pants that are close-fitting from knee to ankle and wider around the hips, originally for horseback riding.

Julian calendar: The calendar system commonly used before the Gregorian calendar. Russia and the Soviet Union followed the Julian calendar (old style) until 1918.

Khrushchev, Nikita (1894–1971): Head of the Soviet Communist Party from 1953 to 1964 and leader of the Soviet Union from 1958 to 1964. He promoted an agenda of de-Stalinization and a liberalization of some Soviet policies.

Khrushchevka: A type of apartment building, inexpensively constructed, commonly erected in the Soviet Union in the early 1960s.

Kirov, Sergei Mironovich (1886–1934): A high-ranking Communist leader who was assassinated in 1934.

kolkhoz: A collective farm.

Komsomol: A Communist youth organization for teens and young adults in the Soviet Union.

kopek: A unit of Russian money, also used in some other Soviet countries. One hundred kopeks equal one ruble.

Kremlin, the: The seat of Russian and Soviet governments and the residence of some Soviet leaders.

kulak: A well-off peasant, persecuted in Soviet Russia.

Lenin, Vladimir (1870–1924): A major political and philosophical leader in the 1917 October Revolution and then the first governmental head of post-revolutionary Russia (1917 to 1924) and the Soviet Union (1922 to 1924). His views provided an important cornerstone for Soviet ideology and, after his death, became known as Leninism.

Leningrad: The name for St. Petersburg from 1924 to 1991.

lifter: An undershirt attached to garters.

Little Octobrists: Soviet children born in 1917, the year of the October Revolution. Also the term used for the Communist youth organization for young children (before they joined the Pioneers).

Lizochek: A diminutive of the name Lisa.

Luxemburg, Rosa (1871–1919): A Polish socialist thinker, writer, and activist.

Marx, Karl (1818–1883): German socialist revolutionary thinker much revered by Soviet leaders; the author of *The Communist Manifesto* (with Friedrich Engels) and *Das Kapital*, among other influential works.

Marxism–Leninism: The combination of Marxist and Leninist philosophies that formed the basis for the Soviet Communist perspective.

May Day: Commonly known as Labor Day in the United States; occurs on May 1 and is a celebration of workers.

Moscow: The capital of Russia and the USSR.

Moscow Trials: A series of large-scale trials during the Great Purge where leaders of the Communist Party were forced to confess themselves as traitors and spies.

muff: A tube, often made of fur, to keep one's hands warm.

Mukhina, Vera (1889–1953): A Soviet sculptor. Her most famous work is *Worker and Kolkhoz Woman*, originally created for the 1937 World's Fair in Paris.

Muscovite: A person who lives in Moscow.

Narkompros: Also known as the People's Commissariat for Education. The Soviet agency in charge of public education.

NEPman: One who engaged in private trade and small business under the New Economic Policy (NEP) from 1921 to 1928.

October Revolution, the (1917): Also known as the Bolshevik Revolution. Led by Vladimir Lenin, the Bolsheviks seize power and inaugurate the Soviet regime.

pantaloons: A type of undergarment.

parasitism: A charge in the USSR accusing someone of not working and benefiting instead from the work of others.

parliament: A legislative body made up of members of varying political parties.

Pasternak, Boris (1890–1960): A poet and novelist; author of *Doctor Zhivago*. He was awarded the Nobel Prize in Literature in 1958 but turned it down for fear of government retribution.

perestroika: A restructuring of Soviet economic policy

that relaxed government control over the economy and allowed for greater independence in the market.

Pioneers: A Communist youth organization for children in the Soviet Union. When the children got older, they joined Komsomol.

pogrom: A violent and deadly attack against a group of people, usually Jews.

Pravda: The Communist Party newspaper; widespread and very influential in the Soviet Union.

proletariat: The working class.

Red Army: The Bolshevik forces in the Russian Civil War (1917–1922) led by Vladimir Lenin. Later used generally to refer to the Soviet armed forces.

Red Square: A central square near the Kremlin in Moscow.

red star: A Communist symbol used widely in the Soviet Union.

rehabilitation: The clearing of one's name in the Soviet Union, sometimes posthumous, after having been accused of and often harshly punished for a supposed crime.

ruble: A unit of Russian money, also used in some other Soviet countries. One ruble equals one hundred kopeks.

Russian Civil War (1917–1922): An internal struggle for power in Russia following the October Revolution. It was fought between the Red Army and White Army.

Russian Constitutional Assembly (1918): An elected body formed after the October Revolution to create a constitution and government for the new Russia; dissolved by the Bolsheviks.

Russian Soviet Federative Socialist Republic (RSFSR): The official name for Russia from 1917 to 1991.

Saint Petersburg: Capital of the Russian empire (pre-revolution) starting in 1712.

Sakharov, Andrei (1921–1989): A nuclear physicist who contributed important work to the Soviet hydrogen bomb and campaigned persistently for human rights in the Soviet Union. He was awarded the Nobel Peace Prize in 1975.

salo: A salted, preserved, fatty pork product popular in Russia and many Eastern European countries.

samizdat: An underground movement consisting of the secret production and distribution of banned literature in the Soviet Union.

samovar: A vessel used in Russia to heat water for tea.

Second Front: The Western front in World War II, beginning with the US invasion of Normandy, France, in 1944, which required the German army to fight in more than one military theater at a time.

Second Patriotic War: A Russian term for World War I.

Seventeen Moments of Spring: A television show about Max Otto von Stierlitz, a Russian spy in Nazi Germany. Stierlitz was immensely popular in Russia and the show had great influence on the country's culture and politics.

shock workers: A prestigious designation for particularly high-achieving or hard-working laborers in the early Soviet Union.

Siberia: A very cold and desolate area that comprised much of the eastern part of the USSR. It was often used as a place of exile and punishment.

socialism: A theory of economics and politics that endorses collective ownership and control of the production and distribution of goods.

Solzhenitsyn, Aleksandr (1918–2008): Russian author of *The Gulag Archipelago* and *A Day in the Life of Ivan Denisovich* whose writing showed real life in the Soviet Union. He was awarded the Nobel Prize in Literature in 1970.

Soviet-Afghan War (1979–1989): A result of the Soviet invasion of Afghanistan in 1979 to aid the communist Afghan government against anti-communist Muslim resistance.

Stalin, Joseph (1878–1953): The authoritarian leader of the USSR from 1924 until his death in 1953, first as the head of the Communist party and then as the premier of the Soviet Union. His time in power was characterized by forced industrialization and increased Soviet influence in addition to brutally repressive policies and widespread executions.

stilyaga: A youth in the Soviet Union who dressed in modern, often Western, clothing.

Thaw, the: The period of increased liberalization under Nikita Khrushchev, beginning in the early 1950s.

trench: A deep ditch used in military engagements during World War I.

Trotsky, Leon (1879–1940): A Communist theorist; an organizer and leader in the October Revolution who was a member of the first post-revolutionary Soviet government. He eventually opposed Joseph Stalin and was exiled from the USSR in 1929, then assassinated in Mexico in 1940 on Stalin's orders.

tsar: The hereditary title of Russian emperors, in power until 1917.

USSR: The Union of Soviet Socialist Republics, also known as the Soviet Union. At its largest, the USSR contained fifteen republics, which would become present-day Armenia, Azerbaijan, Belarus, Estonia, Georgia, Kazakhstan, Kyrgyzstan, Latvia, Lithuania, Moldova, Russia, Tajikistan, Turkmenistan, Ukraine, and Uzbekistan. The USSR had a one-party political system that was dominated by the Communist party.

Vysotsky, Vladimir (1938–1980): A very popular Soviet performer and poet.

White Army: The coalition of forces opposing the Red Army and Communism in the Russian Civil War (1917–1922).

Wilhelm II, Kaiser (1859–1941): The German emperor and King of Prussia during World War I.

World's Fair: An international exhibition of displays from many different countries, showcasing progress in a variety of areas; the first World's Fair was held in London in 1851.

Yeltsin, Boris (1931–2007): The first president of Russia after the dissolution of the USSR.

Select Timeline of Russian/Soviet History (1899–2018)

Some terms and events are further explained in the glossary. (Note: The title of the head of state was not consistent during the Soviet years, so leader is used up until the election of the first president of Russia.)

1899 – Dramatist Anton Chekhov premieres his masterpiece *Uncle Vanya*.

1901 – The Socialist Revolutionary Party is founded. Anton Chekhov premieres *The Three Sisters.*

1904 – Chekhov's *The Cherry Orchard* is first performed.

January 22, 1905 – Bloody Sunday occurs in St. Petersburg.

October 1905 – Tsar Nicholas II issues the October Manifesto, which promises a legislative system whose members would be elected by popular vote.

1909 – Serge Diaghilev founds Ballets Russes in Paris, revolutionizing the art of ballet. The company never performs in Russia.

1910 – Igor Stravinsky composes the ballet *The Firebird* at Ballets Russes.

1913 – Vladimir Tatlin founds constructivism, an art movement featuring abstract elements. Stravinsky composes *The Rite of Spring* at Ballets Russes.

July 28, 1914 – Archduke Franz Ferdinand of Austria is assassinated, sparking World War I.

August 1, 1914 – Russia enters World War I.

February 1917 – The February Revolution occurs in Russia.

November 7, 1917 – The October Revolution (also known as the Bolshevik Revolution) occurs in Russia. The Russian Civil War begins.

1918 – Aleksandr Blok, often regarded as the greatest Russian symbolist poet, writes "The Twelve" in response to the October Revolution.

November 11, 1918 – World War I ends.

August 5, 1920 – Naum Gabo and his brother Antoine Pevsner publish the Realistic Manifesto, a key text of constructivism. The manifesto lays out the brothers' theories of artistic expression in the form of five "fundamental principles" of constructivist practice. The text focuses largely on divorcing art from such conventions as use of lines, color, volume, and mass.

1921 – In early spring, famine strikes Russia, causing the deaths of more than seven million children over the next year.

1922 – Painter Marc Chagall, whose work draws on cubism and Russian folk art, leaves Russia for Paris. Naum Gaubo and Antoine Pevsner also leave Russia.

October 25, 1922 – The Russian Civil War ends.

December 30, 1922 – Vladimir Lenin proclaims the establishment of the Union of Soviet Socialist Republics (USSR).

January 21, 1924 – Vladimir Lenin dies. Soon after, Joseph Stalin becomes leader of USSR.

1925 – Sergei Eisenstein releases *Battleship Potemkin*, winning international acclaim and pioneering the use of montage, a film-editing technique.

January 1928 – Stalin exiles Trotsky and a number of his followers to Alma-Ata, Kazakhstan.

January 1929 – Trotsky is expelled from the Soviet Union.

December 1, 1934 – Sergei Kirov is assassinated.

1936–1938 – The Great Purge (or Great Terror) occurs and many dissenting members of the Communist Party are executed because they are seen as a threat.

September 1, 1939 – World War II begins when Germany invades Poland.

August 1940 – Joseph Trotsky is murdered.

June 22, 1941 – Germany invades Russia, and the USSR joins the war.

May 9, 1945 – Germany formally surrenders. The Soviet Union celebrates the end of World War II (even though Japan will not officially surrender until September).

September 2, 1945 – World War II officially ends when Japan surrenders.

1947 – The Cold War begins between opposing powers in the Eastern Bloc (the Soviet Union and Poland, East Germany, Czechoslovakia, Hungary, Romania, Bulgaria, Yugoslavia, and Albania) and powers in the Western world (the United States, its NATO allies, and others).

March 5, 1953 – Joseph Stalin dies. Georgy Malenkov becomes leader of USSR.

September 1953 – Following a power struggle with Malenkov, Nikita Khrushchev becomes leader of USSR.

February 14–25, 1956 – The Twentieth Congress of the Soviet Communist Party is held, and Nikita Khrushchev's speech denounces Joseph Stalin's dictatorship and cult of personality.

October 4, 1957 – The Soviet Union launches *Sputnik 1*, the first artificial satellite.

1958 – Boris Pasternak wins the Nobel Prize in Literature for his novel *Doctor Zhivago*; his insights into Communist society prompt authorities to force him to refuse the prize.

April 12, 1961 – Soviet Union cosmonaut Yuri Gagarin becomes the first man in space.

October 1962 – The standoff between the United States and the Soviet Union known as the Caribbean Crisis (also known as the Cuban Missile Crisis) occurs.

October 14, 1964 – Khrushchev is ousted from all positions of power. Leonid Brezhnev becomes leader of USSR.

December 24, 1979 – The Soviet–Afghan War begins.

July 19, 1980 – The Soviet Union hosts the opening ceremony for the Summer Olympics in Moscow. The United States is among the many countries that boycott the games because of the Soviet invasion of Afghanistan.

November 12, 1982 – Two days after the death of Brezhnev, Yuri Andropov becomes leader of USSR.

February 13, 1984 – Four days after the death of Andropov, Konstantin Chernenko becomes leader of USSR.

May 8, 1984 – The Soviet Union initiates a boycott of the Summer Olympics in Los Angeles, citing security concerns.

March 11, 1985 – Following Chernenko's death on March 10, Mikhail Gorbachev becomes leader of USSR.

August 19, 1991 – The August Coup, a Soviet coup d'état to take control of the country from Soviet President and General Secretary Mikhail Gorbachev, fails.

December 25, 1991 – The Soviet Union is officially dissolved, and Gorbachev resigns. The Russian Federation (Russia) assumes the rights and obligations of the former Soviet Union.

June 12, 1991 – Boris Yeltsin is elected as the first president of the Russian Federation.

December 25, 1991 – The Soviet Union collapses and the Cold War ends.

December 31, 1999 – Yeltsin resigns and appoints Vladimir Putin president.

May 7, 2000 – Vladimir Putin is officially inaugurated as president.

March 2, 2008 – Dmitry Medvedev is elected president. Putin is appointed prime minister.

April 8, 2010 – The New START treaty, which will reduce the nuclear arsenals of Russia and the United States by half, is signed.

March 4, 2012 – Putin is reelected president (presidential elections will now occur every six years).

February 7, 2014 – Russia hosts the opening ceremony for the Winter Olympics in Sochi.

March 18, 2018 – Putin is again reelected president.

June 14, 2018 – The 2018 FIFA World Cup, held in Russia, begins.

Select Bibliography

Note: Most of the works were originally published in Russia, and some are not easily available in English.

Books

Belovinsky, Leonid, *The Things of the Twentieth Century in Stories and Photographs*. Russia: Rech, 2016.

Kassil, Lev. *The Black Boots and Schwambrania*. Moscow: Progress Publishers, 1978.

Murshova, Ekaterina and Natalia Olgeovna Mayorova. *When My Grandparents Were Small . . .* St. Petersburg: Polyandria, 2016.

Neverov, Alexander. *City of Bread*. New York: Hyperion, 1911.

Journals

The author and illustrator also used a number of contemporary and archival newspapers and magazines for examples of period dress, everyday life, and social and political events. These included *Pravda*, *Pionerskaya Pravda*, *Ogonyok*, *Krokodil*, *Kostyor*, *Pioner*, *Niva*, *Krasnaya Niva*, *Zhensky Jurnal*, and *Rabotnitsa*.

Where to Find the Poems and Songs in This Book

Page 15: "The Twelve," by Aleksandr Blok, 1918. See russiasgreatwar.org/docs/twelve_notes.pdf.

Page 19: "Last Tango" ("In Faraway Steamy Argentina . . ."), lyrics by Iza Kremer, 1914. See youtube.com/watch?v=nqr3zMosHOo.

Page 23: "Two Falcons," lyrics by Mikhail Isakovsky, 1936. See youtube.com/watch?v=Bq1w4t3kFaA.

Page 36: "Fierce and Stubborn," by Bulat Okudzhava, 1946. See samlib.ru/a/alec_vagapov/okud-alldoc.shtml.

Page 40: "Stanzas," by Joseph Brodsky, 1962. The version printed in this book was taken from an original samizdat and differs slightly from the standard version of that poem, as later published. The standard version of the poem can be found in *Collected Poems in English* (New York: Farrar Straus and Giroux, 2002).

Page 41: "We're No Worse than Horace," by Aleksandr Galich, 1966. From *Songs & Poems* (Ann Arbor, MI: Ardis, 1983).

Page 47: "Oh!", lyrics by Natasha Borzhomova (N. Agapova), 1985. See youtube.com/watch?time_continue=4&v=wp-k5pBe4HQ.

Page 47: "A Million Red Roses," lyrics by Andrei Voznesensky, 1981. See poetryrussian.blogspot.com/2014/02/normal-0-false-false-false-en-us-x-none_19.html.

Page 50: "I Want Change," lyrics by Victor Tsoi, 1986. See russmus.net/song/7257#2.

Index

Note: Page numbers in *italics* refer to illustrations.

ЗА НАРОДНОЕ СЧАСТЬЕ,

ДЖЕК·ЛОНДОН
СИЛА
СИЛЬНЫХ

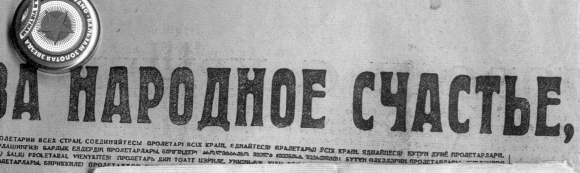

1948

1947

СОВЕТО

СВИДЕТЕЛЬ...
О РОЖДЕН...

ДАША

...ИОНЕР НА КОНЬКАХ ПАВЛУША

Кисловодск 1940.

Пусть дети нарисуют игру в футбол, в лошадки, в крокет, в лапту. Умея уже рисовать, они могут ...рь легко освоиться с любой темой. Нарисовать пионера, комсомолку, красноармейце...